Lucy Clark loves movies. She loves binge-watching box-sets of TV shows. She loves reading and she loves to bake. Writing is such an integral part of Lucy's inner being that she often dreams in Technicolor®, waking up in the morning and frantically trying to write down as much as she can remember. You can find Lucy on Facebook and Twitter. Stop by and say g'day!

Books by Lucy Clark

Mills & Boon Medical Romance

The Lewis Doctors

Reunited with His Runaway Doc

Outback Surgeons

English Rose in the Outback
A Family for Chloe

The Secret Between Them
Her Mistletoe Wish
His Diamond Like No Other
Dr Perfect on Her Doorstep
A Child to Bind Them
Still Married to Her Ex!

Visit the Author Profile page
at millsandboon.co.uk for more titles.

For my babies—
once you were small and now you're grown.
Where did the time go? Thank you for loving me back
and choosing to spend your time with me.

Ecc 7:9

Praise for
Lucy Clark

'A good and enjoyable read. It's a good old-fashioned romance and everything you expect from Medical Romance. Recommended for Medical Romance lovers and Lucy Clark's fans.'

—*Harlequin Junkie* on
Resisting the New Doc In Town

'I really enjoyed this book—well written, and a lovely romance story about giving love a second chance!'

—*Goodreads* on
Dare She Dream of Forever?

P

THE FAMILY
SHE'S LONGED FOR

BY
LUCY CLARK

MILLS
BOON

Published in Great Britain 2017
By Mills & Boon, an imprint of HarperCollins*Publishers*
1 London Bridge Street, London, SE1 9GF

© 2017 Anne Clark

ISBN: 978-0-263-07000-2

Our policy is to use papers that are natural, renewable and recyclable
products and made from wood grown in sustainable forests. The logging
and manufacturing processes conform to the legal environmental
regulations of the country of origin.

Printed and bound in Great Britain
by CPI Antony Rowe, Chippenham, Wiltshire

PROLOGUE

CLARA LEWIS KEPT her head down as she walked to her car. It was close to three o'clock in the morning and her shift in the Emergency Department at Melbourne General Hospital had run very late, but that was the way life was when you were an overworked doctor. She sniffed, telling herself she wouldn't cry—not again, and definitely not within the hospital grounds. Even at this time of the morning she felt as though there were prying eyes, watching her through the darkness.

It wasn't the long hours she spent at the hospital which was upsetting her, it wasn't because the registrar on call had snapped at her, and it wasn't because a patient had decided to share the contents of his stomach all over her shoes. That wasn't the reason she was trying so hard not to burst into tears. No, her reason was the age-old one of a breaking heart. Was it possible to actually *feel* your heart break in two? She hadn't thought so before, but now she most definitely believed it.

Thankfully, Clara made it to the sanctuary of her car and quickly shut the driver's door. After putting the key into the ignition and clipping her seatbelt into place, she gripped the steering wheel and allowed her tears their release. If she bottled up her emotions any more than she already was, she ran the risk of exploding at an unsuspecting person for the most minor infraction.

She wanted to throw back her head and wail, to scream and shout, to share her heartbreak with anyone who cared enough to listen. But at the same time she didn't want anyone to know just how distraught she really was. Clara was well aware of the way the gossips whispered about her as she walked down the corridor. As soon as she came into earshot they would quickly stop and turn their attention to something else, but as soon as she passed them by, off they'd go again.

'How terrible for her.'

'I heard he dumped her at the fundraising dinner.'

'He is so *incredibly* good-looking. Perhaps too good looking for her.'

'I'm not sure what he saw in her anyway.'

'I thought they were just friends. At least they were all through medical school. Some women are meant to stay firmly in the friend-zone rather than trying to chase after a man too good for them.'

That last one she'd heard as she'd been sitting in the cafeteria. The woman who had been gossiping about her had spoken rather too loudly—loud enough for Clara to hear—and even though Clara had tried to rationalise that the gossip might not actually be about *her*, as soon as the gossiper in question had turned and seen Clara sitting there she'd gasped.

'I'm so sorry for what's happened, Clara,' she had mumbled, before scuttling away.

And if it wasn't the whispers in the corridors and back rooms, it was the pitying looks which were shared openly by those staff who knew her. It was getting beyond a joke, and it didn't make working her shifts any easier as it provided a constant reminder of just how Virgil had broken her heart.

At least she only had another fortnight at the Melbourne General until her contract was up. She'd agreed to do a twelve-month specialisation in emergency medicine before taking up a position as junior GP with a busy practice in her home town of Loggeen, forty minutes outside of Melbourne city.

She was looking forward to getting to know her patients, to making sure they weren't just some numbers in a file. She wanted to help people, but apparently Virgil hadn't been able to see that. Now he thought the world of general practice far too mundane for him, and their previous plans to settle down after their internship, and open up a practice together, had evaporated into thin air.

Virgil had fallen in love with general surgery, and the instant he'd changed his preference for the specialisation he'd stopped being the Virgil Arterton she'd come to know and love.

They'd been best friends throughout medical school, and for the past eighteen months they'd been a lot more than friends. Virgil had been accepted onto the service registrar programme before he'd even finished his internship. He was hungry to climb the hierarchical ladder—to become the best general surgeon he could. He was also planning to write his PhD thesis during his registrar training, which Clara had suggested might be a bit foolish.

'You'll be burning the candle at both ends. That won't be good for your health.'

Nor for their relationship, she'd added silently. She hadn't spoken the words out loud because she hadn't wanted to hear him say that their relationship was over. She realised now that all the signs had been there: all the signs that she'd been losing his attention, losing his love, losing his desire to be with her. But she'd ignored them, not wanting to believe that *her* Virgil was like so many of the other egocentric surgeons who walked the hospital corridors.

'I'll be fine.' He'd brushed her concerns away as though her words were nothing more than an annoying fly. 'You could do your PhD with me,' he'd suggested. 'We could both be studying and working together.'

'I'm not interested in doing that.'

And that had been the problem. Virgil had a clear idea of what *he* thought Clara should do with her life, and he wasn't interested in listening to what she had to say.

'I want to be a GP.'

And so the debate had continued between them, until the night when they'd been at a hospital fundraising dinner.

'I was positive you would change your mind during this past twelve months—that you'd agree to do more emergency medicine,' Virgil had told her.

The other thing he'd told her was that he'd been accepted on to the full surgical registrar training programme and would be heading overseas.

'You're not going straight away, are you?'

Clara had felt the nagging pain at the back of her mind, which had been increasing over the past six months, begin to pulse with dread at what he might say next.

'Of course I'm going. It's such an honour—and it's in Montreal. At one of the most ground-breaking hospitals in general surgical medicine.'

'But what about *us*?'

'Clara...' He'd sat back in his chair, his air matter-of-fact. 'We don't want the same things any more. You've made that abundantly clear. Besides, I won't have time for any sort of private life. I'll be constantly at the hospital or studying and brushing up on my French.'

'But what about the other things we've discussed—marriage? Children?'

He'd sighed, as though explaining his plans to an imbecile. 'I'll have no time for any of that. I know that sort of thing is important to you, but it's not my priority—not my focus any more.'

As she'd sat there, watching his mouth move, his words penetrating her heart, she had realised that her Virgil— the man she'd been such close friends with,the man who had once shared all her hopes and dreams for the future— was gone. He was gone, and in his place was an arrogant workaholic.

Yes, she wanted to get married and have children one day, and she'd always thought she'd end up doing that with him. But that wasn't the end of her plans for the future. Clara had hoped that one day she would have her own GP practice—that she'd be a respected member of the community and be known for helping others in their time of need. Wasn't that more important than being the best of the best of the best, with honours?

Shaking her head, Clara sniffed and reached into her bag, hunting for a tissue but finding none. She looked around her car, searching the glove box and other areas for a tissue, or a serviette, or even a piece of paper. Eventually she found an old sticky note, which had a phone number on it written in Virgil's handwriting. She used it to blow her nose.

He'd ended their relationship and the next day he'd flown out to work for a year in Montreal. Clara knew she should be happy he'd shown his true colours—that she hadn't wasted even more years of her life changing her plans to suit his ideals. She'd had a lucky escape.

That had been three weeks ago, and she'd been left to endure the gossips and the pitying looks.

Starting the car's engine, she hiccupped a few times before pulling out onto the road. Thankfully, at this time of the morning, there was little traffic which meant the drive back to her apartment shouldn't take too long.

Determined not to think any more about Virgil while she was driving, she switched on the radio and was trying to find a decent song when out of the blue there were bright lights in front of her...heading straight for her...

Clara braked and tried to swerve, but the last thing she could remember was the sickening sound of crunching metal as two cars collided.

CHAPTER ONE

'CHECK THE LEG PULSE,' Clara Lewis instructed her co-worker, while she continued with chest compressions on their patient.

She'd been working with her retrieval team for almost two years since she'd returned to Australia in time for her brother's wedding. Prior to Arthur tying the knot with her long-time friend Maybelle, Clara had been working in the UK for two and a half years, desperate to forget all about Virgil Arterton. She'd filled those years with meeting new people and getting her life back on track.

'Pulse is present on the left leg, but not on the right.'

'Check for fractures,' she said, before checking her patient's pulse. 'No pulse.'

It was necessary to report all the details to her team to ensure everyone knew the status. That way, they could perform their duties effectively. She continued with chest compressions.

'Possible fracture to the right femur,' Tony stated.

'Pulse!' she called a moment later as the man drew in a staggered breath. 'It's weak, but it's there. Suspected internal bleeding. Geoff—oxygen, stat. Then set up an IV. Push fluids. Tony, deal with the fracture.'

She looked to her patient, a twenty-three-year-old male

who was still unconscious but at least breathing again. She tried calling to him while she checked his pulse once more.

'Hello? Can you hear me?'

No response.

'Pulse is stronger.'

She picked up a stethoscope and checked the man's heart rhythm, pleased with the result.

'Administer an injection of Methoxyflurane to provide pain relief.'

Her team worked together as Tony continued to stabilise the femoral fracture.

'Tony, have we got a pulse in that right leg yet?' Clara performed neurological observations. 'Pupils equal and reacting to light.'

'Right leg pulse is faint, but present,' Tony reported half a minute later.

Once Geoff had the IV set up, Clara dug into her emergency medical backpack for the medication, which was already drawn up and clearly labelled. 'Check medication,' she said to Geoff, who duly confirmed the medication before administering it via the intravenous drip.

Once that was done, Geoff addressed the fracture to the right upper arm, while Clara placed a bandage on a laceration to the left thigh.

Within another five minutes their patient's breathing and blood pressure had stabilised, which meant they were ready to transfer him, with the use of a PAT slide, onto a stretcher and into the waiting ambulance.

Ensuring the man's head was secured in a head and neck brace, and that he was strapped firmly onto the stretcher, they levered him into the ambulance, handing his care over to the paramedics.

Clara shut the doors to the ambulance, then received a round of applause from the crowd. The onlookers, who had been kept away by the barriers, clapped and some even whistled.

'Well done, Dr Lewis. You and your team have successfully stabilised the patient and completed the aims in under the projected time frame.'

Dr Fielding, one of the adjudicators of the retrieval team examination, shook her hand. The entire exercise had been designed not only to test the retrieval teams from different hospitals but also to raise public awareness of the importance of first aid courses.

'If you wouldn't mind delivering the verbal report, we can conclude your proceedings.'

'Thank you, Dr Fielding.'

Clara took a deep breath and looked out at the crowd. She held up her hands for silence and the applause died down.

'I'm Dr Clara Lewis. General Practitioner at the Victory Hospital Specialist Centre, located near Loggeen. This—' she indicated her team '—is RN Tony Simpkin and RN Geoff Thompson, both of whom have trained long and hard in emergency trauma management retrieval procedures.'

There was another round of clapping.

Clara applauded her team as well, then waited for silence. 'Let me state here and now that our patient today was a volunteer from the Melbourne Institute for Dramatic Arts and did a superb acting job. As a team, we were given a medical scenario to follow and we addressed each point in turn. The medications were not really injected into our volunteer and he is perfectly fit and healthy. We thank him for his part in the exercise.'

More clapping.

'Today we were faced with an accident victim who had

sustained a fractured right humerus, which is the bone above the elbow—'

She pointed to the areas on her own body as she listed them.

'Also severe laceration to the left thigh, which involved damaged muscle tissue and a damaged femoral artery, and a minor concussion. But, more importantly, our patient had stopped breathing. After restoring the patient's breathing, through chest compression and oxygen, we were able to stabilise the fractured femoral artery which, if left unattended, can cause a patient to bleed out. The right arm had minor bruises and abrasions, and upon examination it was surmised that the bone was probably broken in at least two places. When the patient was handed over to the paramedics, his breathing, blood pressure and pulse were all stable. His injuries were also stable.'

She paused for a breath, then delivered the point of why these emergency and trauma retrieval scenarios were being played out in the public arena.

'Learning first aid is a valuable asset for each and every person to have. Please,' she implored, 'sign up for a course. The St John's Ambulance and the Red Cross run courses on a regular basis throughout the year. And remember, if *you* were the person lying on the road in need of help, wouldn't you like a passer-by to be trained in first aid so they could help you? *Be* that person. Be that passer-by who could potentially save someone else's life. Sign up today. Thank you.'

She paused as another round of applause broke out.

'Well done again, Dr Lewis,' Dr Fielding reiterated. 'Your team is well trained and your speech was delivered in layman's terms. From checking the preliminary scores of the other adjudicators, I'd say you're in the lead—and with only one more retrieval team to perform, you're in with a good chance.'

'Thank you, Dr Fielding.'

Clara shook the other woman's hand and smiled. As she walked over to her team she glimpsed, out of the corner of her eye, a tall man with jet-black hair walking towards them.

Turning her head sharply in his direction, she recognised him immediately, and felt her heart skip a beat.

'Virgil...'

His name was a disbelieving whisper on her lips. It had been almost six years since she'd last set eyes on him, and she had to admit that, from afar, he looked every bit as handsome as always.

He was wearing navy trousers, a white shirt with rolled up cuffs, a colourful tie and dark sunglasses. Clara didn't need to be told what colour his eyes were. She'd looked into them too many times in the past and lost herself in their depths. Blue. The most compelling and hypnotic blue she'd ever seen.

Shaking the memory away, Clara clenched her jaw, trying to calm her increased heart-rate, needing to get her thoughts onto a more even keel. But her mouth was suddenly dry and a wave of repressed longing washed over her.

Yes, Virgil had broken her heart—but that was in the past. She'd moved on. She'd changed. She wasn't the easygoing Clara of yesteryear. She was a strong, independent woman who had conquered the issues of her past—both emotionally and physically. Still, that didn't mean she had to stick around and talk to people she didn't want to.

'Clara? Are you all right? You've gone pale.'

It was Tony who had spoken, and she looked at her colleague, staring at him blankly for a moment before her mind kicked back into gear.

She forced a smile. 'I'm fine.' She tucked a stray strand

of hair back into the tight bun at the nape of her neck. 'You know, I'm a little thirsty. Do you guys want to get a drink?'

'Uh...I was going to hang around here for a bit,' Tony replied, as he gazed across at some of the nurses who had been part of other teams.

'Yeah, me too,' Geoff added, following Tony's gaze.

'You're both wolves in sheep's clothing,' she retorted good-naturedly.

'And if we win this competition we'll have a lot of those lovely nurses wanting us—not only for our sexy bodies,' Tony continued, 'but also for our brains.'

'Exactly,' Geoff replied. 'We're not just pretty faces.'

Clara shook her head at their antics. 'Fair enough.'

It was good that she was working with men who could make her smile, and yet not feel physically attracted to them.

However, the man who had held her interest for far too many years was most definitely heading her way. When she risked a peek over her shoulder it was to find him bearing down on their location, his strides purposeful and direct.

'Uh...well...I might go. Now. I might go now and get that drink. See you both later.'

'You're not going to wait around for the results?' Geoff called, but she'd already started to walk away and didn't want to stop to answer.

She needed to put as much distance between herself and Virgil Arterton as possible.

He had no idea where she'd disappeared to. One minute Clara had been chatting with the nurses in her retrieval team and the next she'd vanished. Virgil stopped in his tracks and looked around before going to speak to her team.

As one of the adjudicators, he'd known she was going

to be here today, and had been hoping for an opportunity to talk to her. He hadn't wanted to disturb her concentration before she and her team had performed their retrieval exercise, but as soon as it was over, Virgil had made a beeline for her.

He couldn't believe how incredible she'd looked—performing her retrieval, giving her speech. He'd always been attracted to her—even when they'd just been friends throughout medical school—and then, after medical school, when they'd taken their relationship to the next level, he'd gone and ruined everything with his stupidity.

Years ago he'd tried to make contact, to ask her to forgive him, but he'd received no reply. Clearly Clara had been done with him. Now, though—now that he was back in Victoria—he wanted the chance to make things right between them. He wanted to beg her forgiveness, to ask her if it was too late for them to try again.

Although his life had taken several unexpected twists and turns throughout these past years, Virgil had finally figured out what it was he wanted out of life. He wanted Clara back, and he was determined to do everything he could to let her know he'd changed.

'G'day. Dr Virgil Arterton.' He removed his sunglasses and proffered his hand to the two nurses who had been working alongside Clara. 'Well done on your retrieval procedures.'

'Thanks, mate,' Tony replied, noting the badge Virgil was wearing, which declared him to be one of the adjudicators for the retrieval team examinations.

'Uh…I was looking for Clara…er…I mean Dr Lewis.' Seeing the way Tony gave him a concerned look, Virgil added, 'We went to medical school together. I just wanted to catch up and find out how she's doing.'

He shifted his stance, hoping to seem casual as he made the enquiry.

Geoff glanced over his shoulder. 'She was heading to the pub, I think. Said she was thirsty. And the closest place to get a drink is the pub on the corner.'

Virgil followed the direction Geoff was looking. 'Thanks. I'll see if I can catch her up.'

He slipped his sunglasses back into place and walked towards the pub. Had she rushed off because she'd seen him? If that was the case, it clearly meant she didn't want to talk to him. He'd been a jerk all those years ago, full of his own arrogance, his own career, rather than focusing on what was really important in life. And of late, there hadn't been a day that went by when he didn't think about Clara in one way or another.

Sometimes he'd hear an old song on the radio, and it would take him back to when they'd been studying together for their final medical exams, music playing in the background as they'd tried to cram as much information into their brains as possible. Or he'd smell the scent of a greasy diner and remember when they were interns, finishing an excessively long shift at the hospital, and would go for a burger and chips.

Now that he'd returned to the hospital where they'd both once worked—Melbourne General Hospital—the memories came hard and fast. Even the street he was on right now was one he'd traversed with Clara in the past. The pub he was heading to was one where they would often have a drink with all their friends whenever they'd had time off.

When he entered the pub he removed his sunglasses, astonished to find the place as crowded as it had been all those years ago. Several of the people there were medics, either those who were competing in the retrieval examinations or those who had just finished their shift and needed a cold one. At any rate, the front bar of the old Australian pub was crowded.

Was Clara here? If she was, would she be happy to see

him? He hoped so. Yes, their lives had gone along different paths for the last almost six years, but surely that was enough time for her to forgive and forget.

Virgil continued his way towards the bar, rationalising that if Clara wanted a drink that would be the place she'd go. As he politely nudged his way through the throng he saw her. She was standing at the bar, waiting impatiently to be served. He could tell she was impatient by the way she drummed her fingers on the counter—a habit it appeared she hadn't conquered.

A smile touched his face at just how well he'd known this woman in the past. Would she let him get to know her again in the future?

Another woman was beside her, chatting away. Clara was feigning polite interest in between doing her best to attract the bartender's attention. Virgil's smile brightened and his heart filled with anticipation as he neared her location.

He made it to the bar and, as he was tall, drew the immediate attention of the bartender—the same bartender Clara had been trying to get to serve her.

'G'day, mate, what can I get you?' the bartender asked.

'I'll have a beer and...' Virgil paused and glanced down into Clara's upturned face.

At first, she looked annoyed that the bartender was serving someone else before her, but upon seeing just who he was serving she openly gaped in astonishment.

'A lemon squash with a slice of lime?'

It had been her favourite refreshing drink on a hot day. Was he still right? He quirked an eyebrow, waiting for her to respond.

'Actually, I'd like a cranberry juice with sparkling mineral water, please,' she said, after giving Virgil a solid glare, then turned to smile at the bartender. She reached into her pocket for some money.

'It's on me,' Virgil said. 'It's the least I can do.'

He was having a difficult time keeping his mind focused on trying to talk, as even just being this near to her again was causing a tightening in his gut. Nervousness? More than likely. He had a lot riding on this meeting and it wasn't going at all the way he'd planned—probably because her fresh, floral scent was teasing at his senses, reviving even more memories of those intimate times they'd spent together.

Clara shrugged one shoulder, then returned her attention to the woman beside her. 'Sorry, Helen. You were saying...?'

All her attention was on this Helen, which meant none of her attention was on him—or at least that was what she wanted him to think. But he could tell by the way she shifted her body, so there was half a centimetre more distance between them, that she was well aware of his presence.

Helen, however, had a different idea. She looked from Clara to Virgil, then down to Virgil's adjudicator's badge.

'Virgil Arterton? As in *the* Virgil Arterton? The general surgeon who invented a new surgical method which has revolutionised invasive incision procedures?'

Virgil held Clara's gaze for a split second longer before turning to look at Helen. 'You've read my papers?'

'Well, who wouldn't?' Helen asked rhetorically as she held her hand out towards him. 'I'm Helen Simperton. I find your work to be incredibly insightful, as well as revolutionary.'

The bartender had finished making their drinks and, much to Virgil's chagrin, Clara used the excuse of him being trapped by Helen's raptures, to take her drink and leave the bar area.

'What was it that first made you consider changing the

usual way for incising a patient?' Helen asked as Virgil watched Clara almost rush to the other side of the room.

A moment later she disappeared from sight as more people came in through the front doors.

Trying to appear outwardly calm, he sipped his drink and gave Helen brief answers to her questions. He needed to find Clara, to talk to her for more than half a second. It was clear from his reception that she wasn't interested in talking to him, so if he didn't go after her now he might not get another chance until it was too late.

If he were to walk into her consulting rooms at the Specialist Centre and announce that he was the newly appointed general surgeon, she might well resign on the spot—and he didn't want that.

'Will you excuse me, Helen? I need to catch up to Clara.'

Without waiting for Helen to ask another question, he picked up his drink and followed in the direction Clara had gone. He looked in one of the back rooms of the pub, but she wasn't there. He checked another room off to the side. She wasn't there either. Was she in the bathroom? He hovered momentarily outside of the door to the ladies' room, but knew he couldn't barge in there calling her name.

Virgil turned and headed back towards the main bar, and it was then that he spotted half a glass of what looked to be cranberry juice and mineral water sitting on a table near the door. Was it her drink?

He asked some of the people nearby about the drink's owner, and their description matched Clara.

She'd left.

Putting his own drink on the table, Virgil stepped outside into the Melbourne heat. Slipping his sunglasses back into place, he glanced first one way and then the other, and finally spotted her. She was walking briskly down the street, back towards the retrieval teams. When she glanced over her shoulder and saw him standing there, she hastened her pace.

Clearly she was trying to avoid him as much as possible.

Virgil shook his head as he set off after her again, not surprised at her stubbornness. It had been one of those traits which had either endeared her to him, or frustrated him. Today it was the latter. No other woman had ever affected him the way Clara did. She could drive him crazy, make him laugh, and make his heart melt like butter, all within the space of a few minutes. The woman was an enigma, and he'd been captivated by her from the beginning.

With his long strides, he managed to catch up to her just as she was about to cross the road.

'Clara. I need to speak to you. Please?'

She stopped. Sighing heavily, as though admitting defeat, she turned and stared up at him, lifting her arms wide before dropping them back to her sides.

'What do you want, Virgil?'

Now that he was face to face with her—now that he wasn't playing this game of cat and mouse—his mind went momentarily blank, as he stared into her upturned face. Good heavens, didn't the woman have *any* idea just what she did to his insides? That defiant lift of her chin…the way her back and shoulders were rigid, as though preparing for a fight. The way small wisps of her hair escaped their bonds and floated around her face in the warm breeze. *Gorgeous*.

And her eyes, although glaring at him with distrust, were as hypnotic as ever. Why had he been so incredibly stupid in the past? How different their lives might have been if only he hadn't been such a jerk.

'Uh…' He finally managed to stammer the sound, as he shifted his feet and tried to get his brain to work.

'*Uh…?* You've just chased me around the streets of

Melbourne to utter "uh"?' She crossed her arms and angled her head to the side. 'Are you sure it's me you want to speak to, or rather a speech therapist?'

He couldn't help but laugh at her sassiness. She'd always had a sharp wit. 'Oh, Clara. Sweetheart, you haven't changed.'

'Don't call me that.'

'Sorry.' It was then he realised he was wearing his sunglasses and quickly lifted them onto his head. 'OK...' He cleared his throat once again and met her gaze. 'I've been chasing you because I need to tell you something.'

He paused for a second, and again her impatience got the better of her.

'That you're sorry for the way you treated me all those years ago?'

'Well...there's that—and I am deeply sorry—' His words received an eye-roll from her. 'But, more importantly, I wanted to let you know that I've returned to Melbourne.'

'I can see that. You're standing right in front of me,' she retorted.

'To live,' he added.

There was a moment of silence between them as she processed his words. 'You'll be working at Melbourne General?'

'Uh...no... Well...when I say I've returned to Melbourne, I mean I'm going to be living in Loggeen.'

'What?'

'And...working at Victory Hospital... and at the Specialist Centre.'

At his words, her expression changed from one of impatient annoyance to one of horrified disbelief. Then she closed her eyes and shook her head.

'No, you're not.'

'Yes. I am. I start there in two weeks' time.'

'Then you can *un*-start. Get out of your contract. Take

a different job. Anywhere. Anywhere but at *my* hospital and *my* specialist centre. *No!*'

Her words were firm, direct, and yet he detected a hint of desperation—as though she *really* did not want him anywhere near her. Did she hate him that much?

'I've already bought a house in the district.' He cleared his throat. 'We start moving in tomorrow.' His words were rolling from his mouth quite fast. 'I wanted you to hear this from me, not from any gossip or the rumour mill.'

'*We?*'

She clenched her jaw, and a moment later he could have sworn he saw her eyes brim with tears. Were they tears of anger or tears of joy? He hoped it was the latter, but was pretty sure it was the former.

Clara immediately looked down at the ground, as though she were wishing it would open up and swallow her. When she spoke her voice was polite. Too polite. And when she lifted her head, she didn't quite meet his gaze.

'Thank you for letting me know, Dr Arterton.'

With that, she turned and continued on her way back to her retrieval team.

Virgil wanted to call out to her—to let her know where he'd be living, to invite her to dinner so she could meet his daughter. He wanted to gather her into his arms and never let her go. He wanted to rectify the mistakes from his past, to ask for forgiveness and beg her to give him another chance. Even the small amount of time he'd spent in her company had reignited the desire he'd had for her in the past. Of course he did none of that, because her reception of him had shown him exactly where he stood— far, far away from her.

The hopes he'd had, the plans he'd made, the way he'd wanted to find a way to get her back into his life, had all come crashing down.

Clara hated him.

CHAPTER TWO

'TODAY I THINK I'll have...' Clara surveyed the mouthwatering row of different fudges, trying to decide. 'Peppermint chocolate.'

'Coming right up.' Marni cut the fudge and placed it into the mixer.

This was Clara's favourite time of the day. She watched as Marni operated the machine that would mix the ice-cream with the fudge, producing the most scrumptious taste Clara had ever experienced.

'There you go.'

Marni handed over the small bowl filled with the dessert and Clara paid.

'Thanks.'

Clara eyed the dish she now held so protectively in her hand. As always, she would have at least one spoonful before leaving the shop. She swirled the spoon around the edge of the bowl and scooped some up. Her lips parted in anticipation and the spoon slipped between them.

Clara closed her eyes. 'Mmm...' She could feel her body begin to relax from the pressures of her rigorous medical practice. 'Heaven!'

The small pieces of the fudge mixed with the smooth, creamy ice-cream as she swirled them around in her mouth before swallowing.

'It really is the small things in life that can bring you so much joy.'

Marni laughed. 'Enjoy. I'll see you later.' She moved off to serve other customers.

As Clara stepped out of the shop, she heard one of the new customers saying, 'What was she eating? It looked delicious.'

Taking slow steps, she placed another spoonful into her mouth, then stopped at the kerb to enjoy the flavours. There were at least thirty different varieties of fudge at Marni's shop, and Clara had sampled each and every one of the them at least fifty times over.

She was so busy focusing on her delicious dessert that she almost walked into a man pushing a pram with a toddler in it, and the pregnant woman beside him. The woman looked to be in her second trimester, and the pang of envy which always ripped through Clara when she saw a pregnant woman came swift and fast.

She skirted around the young family, neatly avoiding the collision, and scooped another spoonful into her mouth, willing the sensation to calm the feeling of emptiness she'd carried with her for almost six years.

She would never be able to give birth to a child.

She pressed the button for the pedestrian crossing, eating more ice-cream while she waited for the lights to change. And then she saw him. Virgil Arterton. So he had come. He was here. He was back in Loggeen and he would be working at the Specialist Centre and Victory Hospital.

She'd held out a vain hope that after their brief conversation in Melbourne he would change his mind, that somehow a strange twist of fate would cause his plans to be altered.

When she'd returned to Loggeen after the retrieval exercise, she'd checked with her colleagues and discovered that Virgil had spoken the truth. The two of them would be working in the same building as well as the same hospital.

Thankfully, their paths shouldn't cross when she was doing her twice-monthly stints in the Emergency Department at Victory Hospital, given that Virgil was a qualified general surgeon and would be using the hospital to hold public clinics and operate on his patients. In fact, she was hopeful that their paths would rarely cross, and that when they did they would be able to nod politely to each other and go about their business.

Gone were the days when she had pined over him. Clara was in control of her own future, and right now she was more than happy with the way her life was turning out. Good general practice, helping people at the Specialist Centre and in the ED, as well as going out with the retrieval teams when necessary. Her family lived close—her brother and his family even lived in the same building as her—and although her parents were presently overseas, enjoying another long cruise, the Lewis family was a close-knit one.

Yes, she was more than happy with her life—and, as such, there was absolutely no room for Virgil Arterton in it.

A car horn beeped, bringing her out of her reverie. It was then she realised that the light had turned green, indicating it was safe for her to cross the road, but like a ninny she'd simply stood there, speculating about Virgil, while a bowl of ice-cream and fudge melted in her hand.

Crossing the street, she walked up the paved pathway to the doors of the Specialist Centre. After they'd whooshed open, Clara continued walking through the lobby to her consulting rooms. Pushing open the glass door, she was met by her ever-smiling receptionist, Jane.

'You'll never guess who was just in here!' she gushed as Clara placed her bowl on the desktop.

'The King of Persia?' she growled, preoccupied with her anger.

Now she had one more thing to add to her dislike of *'him'*. One glimpse of Virgil Arterton and she'd lost all enjoyment of the confection she loved so much. She spooned some more into her mouth, hoping to recapture the sensations again. *Nothing.*

'Oh, what flavour did you get today?' Jane asked, eyeing the greenish tinge to the ice-cream. 'Peppermint chocolate,' she guessed, before Clara could say a word. 'I thought you had that last week?'

'Does it matter?' Clara snapped, then immediately apologised. 'I'm sorry, Jane. When's my next patient due?'

'You've got another ten minutes before Mrs Holden comes in.'

Clara walked through to her office and put the bowl on her desk. 'Coffee?' she asked Jane.

'Sure—if you're getting some.'

'Hey, I've got ten whole minutes to spare and I've got the best dessert in the world sitting on my desk. I may as well go the entire way and have a hot cup of coffee instead of sculling a lukewarm one.'

'Talk about spoilt.' Jane grinned. 'Oh, I forgot to tell you who was here. The most dashingly handsome and gorgeous man I've ever seen in my life. He was really tall—about six feet four inches, I'd say—with the most wonderful thick black hair that I could just run my fingers through for ever, and—'

'Hypnotic blue eyes?' Clara finished, trying desperately to ignore the way the description was permanently burned into her memory. She shook her head, annoyed with herself for describing his eyes as 'hypnotic'. Why hadn't she just said 'blue'? 'Virgil Arterton.'

'You *know* him?' Jane's eyebrows rose to meet her fringe.

'You could say that.' Clara shook her head dejectedly and sighed. 'Milk, no sugar—right?'

'Yeah. But, Clara…'

Clara didn't wait to be questioned. She stalked to the communal kitchen, which was shared by the staff at the medical centre, and started to make coffee for herself and Jane.

Cedric Fowler, the local obstetrician, was sitting at the table with a smile on his face.

'You look happy, Cedric,' Clara stated.

'Our new general surgeon was just in here. Actually, he asked after you.'

'He did?' Dread instantly washed over her. 'Why? What did you say? You didn't tell him anything, did you? Did you tell him I wasn't here?'

The words tumbled out of Clara's mouth, her eyes wide with a mixture of fear and annoyance.

It wasn't that she was afraid to see Virgil. Rather, she was sceptical about working in such close proximity with him. She needed Virgil to be professional about their relationship—not blab about their past to all and sundry. She'd done everything she could to move forward with her life, to put her past behind her, and the last thing she needed was Virgil digging it up again, telling people they'd been a couple, reigniting the old gossip.

'Uh…' Cedric eyed her in confusion. 'You *weren't* here, Clara. Besides, didn't the two of you used to know each other? I thought you were at med school together?'

Darn Cedric and his perfect memory. 'Yes. Yes, we were close friends. And then we weren't—aren't.'

Cedric's frown increased. 'I hope whatever it is that exists between the two of you won't interfere with—'

'We're both professionals, Cedric,' Clara interrupted, reassuring him.

'Good, because we need Virgil here consulting as our resident general surgeon. We're lucky to have a man as widely published as him agree to come to Victory Hospital.'

Clara smiled politely at Cedric and nodded once more. She'd grasped his meaning. GPs like her were found everywhere—yet established and successful surgeons like Virgil usually worked at larger hospitals in capital cities, not in smaller cities or outer suburbs.

'There'll be no drama between Virgil and myself,' she promised as she returned her attention to making coffee.

'That's good to know,' a deep voice said from the doorway.

Clara immediately closed her eyes as an unbidden wave of desire swept through her at the sound of Virgil's modulated tones. Darn the man! She hadn't even looked at him and already her body was betraying her. Well that was OK, she quickly rationalised. It was OK to be attracted to him—after all, he *was* a good-looking man. However, she knew the real Virgil—the man behind the façade—and she knew there was no way she'd ever be able to trust him again. Therefore the attraction, and the way he could cause goosebumps to tickle their way across her skin with the sound of his voice, meant nothing. *Nothing!*

'Ah, Virgil, you've returned,' Cedric said. 'You didn't forget anything, did you?'

'No.'

Clara could hear the two men shaking hands.

'Just needed a quick word with Clara.'

'Right. I'll leave you to it,' Cedric said, before exiting the small room and closing the door behind him.

Clara felt completely trapped. She was standing at the bench where the coffee things were and Virgil was near the door. There was a table and chairs between them. She didn't want to be here. She didn't want to see him. She most certainly didn't want to talk to him. But what she wanted didn't matter.

Cedric was right. The Specialist Centre needed Virgil to consult here. It would allow a lot of patients to have their surgeries at Victory Hospital rather than having to travel to Melbourne for treatment. She needed to be professional. She needed to be cool, calm and collected. She could do it. She could work alongside the man who had broken her heart and shattered her world to pieces. She was strong. She was different now. *She could do this.*

Turning slowly, she consciously unclenched her jaw and wrapped a mental shield around herself. The Arterton charm had been known to break through all the barriers she could erect, and she had vowed never to leave herself that vulnerable again.

Their eyes met and held for a second. Jane's description of him had been accurate. He was devastatingly handsome. He was dressed in denim jeans and a white polo shirt. His hair was as dark as midnight, with a hint of grey at the temples, but it was his lovely blue eyes that had always been able to make her knees go weak and her heart skip a beat.

'Clara.' Virgil smiled. 'Good to see you again.'

She nodded in his direction, but didn't return his smile. 'Virgil.'

Considering his presence had once again shaken her foundations, she was pleased that at least her voice sounded calm and controlled.

'Can I talk to you a moment, please?'

Clara closed her eyes and shook her head. 'What do you want, Virgil?' The question was soft, but she knew he'd heard her.

'I wanted to make sure you were OK with me working here.'

'It's a bit late to consider my feelings now.'

'True,' he acquiesced as he sat at the table. 'But had I given you a choice—if I'd run my plans by you—chances are you would have said no, you *didn't* want me working here.'

'Well, you're here now,' she stated as she crossed to the fridge and removed the milk.

She was positive she could feel his eyes watching her every move. The subtle sway of her hips beneath the navy cotton skirt. The rigidity of her spine under the light blue shirt.

With her back still to him, she asked, 'Just out of curiosity, what *are* your reasons for moving here?'

She collected two cups and spooned in some instant coffee and sugar. The actions were automatic, but after putting three sugars into her own cup, when she usually only had one, she knew she wasn't concentrating on anything but awaiting Virgil's response.

'Well...besides wanting to be nearer to you and to spend time with you—'

'Whoa!' She turned to face him, teaspoon upheld in her hand. 'Wait a second. *Nearer* to me? Spend *time* with me? What planet are you living on?' She scowled. '*You* may be quite comfortable cheating on your wife, but I am most definitely *not* happy to be "the other woman"—so you can forget about it.' She shook the teaspoon at him as though that would help to prove her point.

'How did you know I was married?'

'I bumped into Misty Fox from med school about three years ago. She told me that you'd got married—which surprised me, because I was pretty sure one of the reasons we broke up was because you didn't want to get married and have a family. You wanted to focus on your career. You didn't want me cramping your style.'

'I never said that last bit.'

'It was implied. So clearly your career's going well, *and* you found someone you wanted to marry, so why on earth would you want to spend more time with *me*?'

'Clara, can we sit down and just talk?'

'No. I have a clinic and I need to make coffee for myself and Jane.' She busied herself with adding hot water to the cups and starting to stir them.

'I'm not married.'

He seemed to blurt out the words and she glared at him over her shoulder.

'You just told me you were!'

'No. I asked how you knew I was married.' He shook his head and stood. 'I'm a widower.'

'Oh.' She slowly exhaled, the anger she'd been holding so close starting to wane a little. 'I'm sorry, Virgil. That must be difficult for you.'

'She died in a car accident—with her lover.'

'Oh!'

Car accidents… They really had a way of changing things.

'Clara, it's true my career is going great—so great that I can choose where I want to go. And I've chosen to come back to my old stomping ground of Loggeen.'

'But why? Seriously, it can't be because of me—so why?'

'It's a great place to raise a family.'

'You have *children*!'

She couldn't believe the pain that pierced her heart at this news. Not only had he broken her heart all those years ago, declaring he didn't want to be with her because he needed to focus on his career, but the reasons he'd given—that he didn't want to get married and have a family—meant the truth of the matter was that he hadn't wanted to have those things with *her*.

Clenching her jaw, she tried to keep her voice neutral. She'd promised Cedric that she would be professional, and by golly she was going to be as professional as possible.

'I'm very happy you've chosen to raise your family here. It is a great part of the country, with a lot of good schools.'

'I have one child, Clara. Her name is Rosie and she's three years old, so not quite ready for school.'

'And you've moved her here because…?' She tried hard to keep the pain from her voice.

'Because she's young enough to make a fresh start.'

'I see. Well, I hope you'll be very happy working here at the Specialist Centre.' She picked up the coffee cups, holding them in front of her like a barrier. 'As far as we're concerned, I think it's best if we just forget the past and continue on like the professionals we are.' She took a step forward. 'Would you mind opening the door for me, please?'

'Don't be like this.'

She forced a smile. 'Like what?'

'Like…like an automaton.'

Clara sighed with exasperation. She was standing near the door and so was he. It had been a mistake to move closer to him, because now all her senses were attuned to every little thing about him. The scent surrounding him was the same spicy aura she'd always equated with him.

'So you're really going to be working here?' Her words were barely a whisper.

He edged a little closer to her. 'Afraid so.'

His breath fanned her neck. She could feel her body respond to his closeness, even though he wasn't touching her. Clara tried to control not only her breathing but her wayward emotions as well. How was it that whenever he got within coo-ee of her, every sense went on alert, every fibre of her being became attuned to his every move.

'You've cut your hair,' he stated, his voice still soft. 'The last time I saw you it was almost down to your waist.'

'It needed cutting.'

'It looks good shoulder-length. Professional.'

Clara fought against his deep, sensual tone. It washed over her like silk, making her feel vulnerable.

'I've always loved the colour. Rich, dark brown—to match your eyes.'

Clara sucked in her breath at his words. Her whole body seemed to be tingling with awareness at his close proximity. Although he wasn't touching her, she could feel the warmth his body exuded and it enveloped her like a glove. How was it that after all this time—after all the therapy she'd undergone both physically and emotionally—he could still affect her in such a way? Did she *really* have no self-control where he was concerned?

'Clara!'

A female voice called from the distance, breaking the small bubble surrounding herself and Virgil. Clara almost spilt the coffees at hearing Jane's voice.

'Quick, open the door,' she stated.

He rested his hand on the doorknob, but paused. 'Do you have patients now?'

'Yes—and you've just completely ruined the only ten minutes I've had to myself all day.'

'Are you free for dinner tonight?'

'No.'

'Tomorrow night?'

'No.'

'But we need to talk, Clara. We need to sort things out.'

'Will you please just open the door?'

'The next night?'

'*Yes*. Just open the door!'

With a goofy grin at her acceptance, he opened the door just in time for Clara to see Jane walking towards the kitchenette.

'I knew you'd get sidetracked,' her receptionist said. 'Mrs Holden's here.'

Without seeing Virgil on the other side of the kitchenette door, Jane took the coffee Clara had made and immediately took a sip.

'If you don't hustle, you'll be running late,' Jane remarked as she turned and headed back the way she'd come.

Clara looked up at Virgil in disdain. 'That was a dirty trick and there's no way you can hold me to that acceptance.'

'Yes, I can.'

'No, you can't. Agreeing to have dinner with you was the only way I could get you to open the door. Desperate times sometimes call for desperate measures.'

'I completely agree—which is why I had to trap you into dining with me.'

'Aha! So you admit it was a trap.'

Virgil smiled widely at her words. 'I've missed this, Clara. This crazy banter we used to share.'

And so had she, but she wasn't going to admit it.

'Please—have dinner with me some time before I officially start next Monday. Sunday night would be good for me, if it's good for you.'

Sighing, she knew she wasn't going to get her Friday afternoon clinic done unless she agreed. 'Fine. Sunday night.'

'I'll email you the details.'

'OK. My email address is—'

'I have a list of everyone's email here at the Specialist Centre,' he told her, then took her free hand in his and brought it to his lips, pressing a soft and sweet kiss to her knuckles. 'Until Sunday.'

'Ugh!' She jerked her hand free and rolled her eyes at his corny action, then headed towards her consulting room.

She made sure she walked in a calm and controlled manner down the corridor, once again feeling his gaze watching her movements. The effects from that gentle kiss on her hand had sent a wave of wildfire spreading throughout her body. It *had* to be wrong that she was still this attracted to him, right?

Placing the now lukewarm coffee on her desk, she looked at the melted bowl of ice-cream and fudge. That was exactly how she felt. Once upon a time she'd been the most important person in Virgil's life. Then visions of being the best in his profession, of working all the time and spending little or no time with the people who mattered most, had become his main focus. And she'd been discarded—shoved aside as though she were nothing but a distant memory.

'Why did he have to come back?'

The question was spoken to her empty consulting room, the words filled with pain from the past and desperation for the future. If he'd affected her this strongly just by being in the small kitchenette with her, how on earth was she supposed to cope dining with him on Sunday evening?

What she needed to do was to prescribe herself a healthy dose of living in the present and ignoring the past—and a double dose of self-preservation.

CHAPTER THREE

Virgil sat on his bed on Sunday evening, amazed at how nervous he was about actually sitting down to talk to Clara face to face. They'd been friends for such a long time during medical school—studying together and buoying each other up, especially around exam time. Several times they'd discussed whether or not they should change the nature of their relationship.

'If we do that,' Clara had rationalised once, 'if we become *more* than friends, what happens if we have a fight? I need you to help me through these next few years, Virgil. You're my study partner, my lab partner, my cheer team—just as I'm yours.'

'You're right,' he'd agreed. 'That's far more important at the moment.'

'And, besides, who knows what might happen if we change the dynamic? What if we don't like kissing each other?'

'We're only going to find out if we try,' he'd encouraged, too embarrassed to tell her how he hadn't been able to stop thinking about it. They were friends, and he hadn't wanted to ruin that friendship by taking their relationship to the next level.

They'd been sitting in one of the back corners of the Loggeen City Library, studying for a coming practical exam. Several medical texts had been scattered between the two of them, and Virgil had been leaning on the table, his elbow almost knocking one of the books off as he propped up his head.

Clara had stared at him for a moment, looking severely tempted. And after a long moment of contemplation, of staring longingly at each other's mouths, wondering and wishing, it had been Clara who had broken the tension surrounding them, shaking her head and tapping the text in front of him.

'Let's just focus on learning the anatomy of the abdomen, so when we dissect the cadaver we actually know what we're doing.'

And that had been the end of the discussion—until the next time the subject had arisen. The following time it had been *his* turn to be the strong one and again insist that they remain friends.

'At least until medical school is over and done with.'

When they had finally been done with studying, he wasn't sure who had been more surprised—himself or Clara—at the way they'd congratulated each other, wrapping their arms around each other, their lips melding in perfect synchronicity.

'Oh, it's *there*,' he'd breathed triumphantly against her lips. 'I knew it would be.'

'Shut up and kiss me,' she'd ordered, and he'd willingly complied.

Now, raking a hand through his hair, Virgil exhaled and stood, walking over to the tallboy in his bedroom, which was adorned with framed photographs of his daughter. He reached into the top drawer and pulled out a bundle of other photographs from the back—photographs of himself and Clara. Her hair was pulled back into a long braid in most of them, although there were one or two where her hair was loose. He'd always loved to run his fingers through those gorgeous locks.

He flicked through the photos, and stopped at what had been the last photo of them taken together. They'd been attending a fundraising dinner for the Melbourne General Hospital's cancer centre. A professional photographer had taken their picture at the table. Even though they'd pasted on their smiles, looking at Clara now, he could see just how unhappy he'd made her.

'This has been going on for months,' she'd told him earlier that night. 'You're always at the hospital—even when you don't need to be. If you don't slow down you're going to end up sick from exhaustion.'

'Just because *you* don't have any desire to specialise, and are more than happy to be a GP for the rest of your life, it doesn't mean you should criticise *me* for chasing my dreams. I want to be a general surgeon. Do you know how difficult it is to get onto the training programme, Clara? I've managed that after only doing one year as a service registrar. *One year.*'

He'd spread his arms wide.

'And now I've been accepted to go and train overseas for the next twelve months—again, for a first-year registrar that is almost unheard of, and yet they've chosen *me.*'

'I'm very happy for you, but—'

'*Are* you? Or are you completely jealous of my success?'

He'd fixed her with a stare that had indicated he wouldn't believe a word that came out of her mouth, because as far as he had been concerned, she was the biggest liability in his career plan.

'Perhaps it's best if we take a break from each other while I'm overseas. I think you were right all those years ago when we were in medical school—we should never have changed the nature of our friendship. At least now that you're done with your training, you don't need me to hold your hand any longer.'

Virgil closed his eyes at recalling the words his past self had sprouted to Clara. How *could* he have treated her in such a fashion? He'd been so full of his own self-importance, so determined to succeed, that he'd pushed away the one person who had always been there for him, who had always shared in his successes.

It had been almost eight months into his overseas placement in Montreal, after he'd presented a paper and received an award, that he'd realised he had no one special to share it with. What had been worse was that when he'd tried to contact Clara to apologise, he'd received no response.

'She's giving you a second chance tonight,' he told his reflection sternly. 'Don't blow it.'

The knock at his bedroom door made him turn to see Gwenda standing in the doorway, looking at him with a small smirk on her face.

Gwenda had been an old friend of his mother's, and after she'd nursed her husband through terminal cancer she'd been at a loose end, her children all grown with lives of their own. When Virgil had found himself a widower, with a six-month-old daughter to care for, as well as a full workload, Gwenda had offered to help out as his live-in housekeeper and nanny.

'I'm nervous,' he told her.

'You'll be fine.'

'What if she doesn't show up?'

'What if she *does*?'

'What if she refuses to listen to what I have to say?'

'What if she *doesn't*?'

Virgil closed his eyes. 'I hope she listens. I hope so much that Clara and I can patch things up.'

'Rosie's ready for bed. Go and say goodnight, then off you go to get some answers to these questions.'

Virgil opened his eyes and smiled at the mention of his daughter. 'Good plan.'

He'd thought about asking Clara to come to his house for dinner and meet Rosie, but they really did have a lot to discuss. They needed to try and put the past in the past and hopefully forge a future together. At least that was what *he* wanted. Was he being foolish putting all his cards on the table?

As he went through the nightly routine with his gorgeous girl, checking her teeth and reading her stories, Virgil embraced the love he felt for his daughter. Rosie didn't judge him—she simply loved him because he was her daddy. That innocent, unconditional love had been the starting point for his present plan. Being upfront and honest with Clara was the only way he knew how to try and win her back.

Clara arrived way too early at the restaurant, but she wanted to be there when Virgil arrived. She wanted to show him that she was a different person from the one he'd known all those years ago—the woman who had run late for dates, late for classes and late for everything in between. Now she was a successful GP, with her own thriving practice. She was well respected by her peers and within her community. She was happy, content, and she didn't need a boyfriend from her past to insinuate himself back into her life.

The problem was that Virgil wasn't *just* an old boyfriend. He'd been the true love of her life, and long before their relationship had changed from one of friendship to one that was much, much more, Clara had been in love with him. However, as she constantly reminded herself, the past was the past—and regardless of what Virgil had planned for his move back to his old stomping ground, it definitely wouldn't be including her. Not in a romantic light anyway. Professional colleagues she could cope with. Nothing more.

Finally he arrived, ten minutes before their appointed time. She saw his eyebrows rise when the maître d' indicated that Clara was already there. She watched as he walked towards the table, his stride sure and steadfast. She liked the way he walked. She'd liked watching him walk in the past, and now was no exception.

It wasn't until he stood before her that she realised she'd been staring.

'Shall I add a little pivot for you?' He quirked his eyebrow, his gaze filled with memories of the past, his lips pulled into an intriguing smile.

It wasn't the first time he'd asked her that question, but she was determined tonight would be the last. Ignoring the way his smile had caused a flood of tingles to invade her body, and the way his spicy scent teased her senses, she indicated a chair.

As he sat, he continued to smile. 'You're early!'

'I've changed, and I want you to know that I'm not interested in picking up the threads of our old relationship.'

'Straight to the point. Good.' He opened the menu and glanced at it for a whole three seconds before declaring, 'Well, I know what I'm having. How about you?'

'Yes.'

'Excellent.'

He summoned a waiter and they gave their orders.

Once they were alone, he shifted in his chair before leaning forward. 'Thank you for agreeing to dine with me.'

'As far as I'm concerned, Virgil, it's merely a strategy to ensure we can keep the past where it belongs and work alongside each other like professionals.'

'I couldn't agree more.'

Upon hearing those words, Clara sighed. 'Good.'

He was going to see sense. Thank goodness for that.

No more talk of moving back to Loggeen just so he could see her again. Clara picked up her glass of water and took a sip. Perhaps this dinner wouldn't be so bad after all.

'But that doesn't mean we can't investigate whether or not there are any residual feelings remaining from our past relationship,' he continued.

She accidentally sprayed some of her mouthful of water on him, before choking on the rest as she swallowed the wrong way. Coughing and spluttering, she was powerless to stop him from patting her on the back in an effort to ease the obstruction.

'Steady on.' He picked up a napkin and dabbed at where the water had landed.

'I didn't mean to spit on you,' she remarked between coughs.

Virgil chuckled. 'Just like old times. The two of us having fun together.'

Clara gave one last cough, then shook her head. 'No, Virgil. It's not. It can never be like old times again.'

She tried to make her words sound firm, definite, but her throat was still recovering from the coughing spasm and therefore sounded a little croaky.

'As we're speaking frankly, I've got to ask why you won't even consider it.' He went to reach for her hand but she shifted back in her chair. Virgil looked at both his own hands for a moment before saying softly, 'I've changed too, Clara. I really have. I'm not the idiotic moron I was back then. I apologise for what I said and for the way I treated you.'

Clara pondered his words for a long moment. 'Thank you for apologising.' She tilted her head to the side and aimed her next question at him. 'So what are you planning? To waltz back into my life, woo me once more and then—what?'

He held her gaze, his tone filled with conviction. 'Then

we fall in love again. Marriage. Children. Careers. Happy families until death do us part.'

Clara openly gaped at him in astonishment. 'And you told me you'd changed.' She shook her head. 'What absolute rubbish!'

'I *have* changed, Clara.'

'Really? Hmm…let's review. In the past you wanted to break up with me, head overseas and focus on your career. Check.' She mimed the act of making an imaginary tick in the air. 'Then you decided to get married and have children.' She mimed another tick. 'Check. Then things didn't turn out exactly as you planned so you thought, *Hmm… Clara wanted to marry me in the past, so I think I'll return to Loggeen and pick up where we left off. I'll wine and dine her, I'll woo her, and she'll remember what we once had. I'll tell her I've changed. I'll apologise for the pain I caused and then everything will be fine.*'

Clara twisted her napkin beneath the table, the piece of material receiving a good portion of her pent-up frustration.

'It's always what *you* want, Virgil. *Your* career. *Your* plan. You haven't changed one bit and I'm not falling for you again.'

'But I *have* changed,' he said imploringly, his words urgent. Even his facial expression showed he thought he spoke the truth. 'I'm not as selfish as I was before. I've learned, Clara. I really have learned how to put others first.'

She laughed with disbelief. 'Really?'

'Yes.'

'So why didn't you *ask* me? Why didn't you take my feelings into consideration before barrelling your way back into my life?'

'You would have said no.'

'And I'm still saying no.' Clara twisted the napkin

tighter as she tried to hold on to her frustrations. 'You never listened in the past and you're not listening now, Virgil. I don't *want* to renew our past relationship. I'll work alongside you. I'll be professional and friendly. But nothing more.'

She paused and swallowed, focusing on her breathing in an effort to get her emotions under control. He didn't venture any comment and she was pleased about that. She needed to say what she'd come here to say and then she could leave—could return to her apartment, hug her dog and cry over what might have been for the very last time.

'I can't do this, Virgil. I can't do "you and me" again. It almost killed me last time—literally—and it's taken me years to get to where I am now. I just can't do it.'

Clara was certain the napkin in her hands was about to break, she was twisting it so much. Now that she'd told him how she felt—now that he could be sure there was no future for the two of them—she wasn't sure whether she should stay and wait for her meal or simply leave. However, she didn't want to leave him to pay for her meal. One of the other ways she'd changed was in taking care of herself. She was an emancipated woman and she liked it.

Deciding it was best to leave and pay for her uneaten meal on the way out, Clara shifted her chair back slightly to make her exit easier. It had been a whole fifteen seconds since she'd finished talking, and he hadn't made any comment.

'I'm sorry to skip out on dinner,' she stated as she started to rise from her chair, the napkin still in her hands. 'But I think it's best if I go.'

'What do you mean our break-up almost killed you *literally*? What—what happened?'

Clara's eyes widened in surprise. For some reason she'd thought he'd know about her accident, but how could he? It wasn't as though they moved in the same circles, except for bumping into the occasional friend from medical school, like Misty Fox.

'Oh. I guess you wouldn't know, would you?'

'Wouldn't know what?'

Clara sat back in her chair and met his gaze across the table. 'It was three weeks after you left for Montreal. I was involved in a horrific car accident.'

Virgil stared at her, his mouth dropping open slightly. 'Clara...' He shook his head. 'I didn't know.'

'How could you? You'd left.'

'That's unfair.'

'Granted,' she acquiesced. 'I was heading home from the hospital and a drunk driver side-swiped my car. I was in a bad way—pelvic fracture, lots of operations, lots of intensive therapy which lasted the better part of a year—and once I was back on my feet again I headed overseas myself for a few years.'

'Why did you go overseas?'

She closed her eyes and rubbed her forehead. 'Because of my parents...because of Arthur.'

She opened her eyes and looked at him, locking the memories away before they could take hold. Whenever she'd thought about the accident in the past, she'd usually ended up with a terrible migraine and a sleepless night.

'They all gave up so much for me. I moved back home. Mum looked after me. Arthur drove me to rehabilitation. Dad paid my hospital bills when my savings ran out. They all gave and gave and gave.'

'Probably because they love you.'

'And that's why I needed to go away—not only to try and find myself, to heal myself emotionally and mentally, but to give them all a break. I came back in time for Arthur's wedding.' She smiled when she thought of her brother and his lovely wife Maybelle. 'He's so happy.'

'I'm glad for Arthur—but what about you? Are *you* happy?'

Virgil's words were soft and caring, creating the beginnings of an intimate bubble between them.

Clara met and held his gaze. 'Yes.'

'*Really* happy? Not just happy enough?'

'Virgil…'

She sighed, trying not to lose herself in the depths of his wonderful eyes. She could see his concern for her— could see that he was genuinely interested in her answer. *Was* she happy?

'I'm content with my life. I like things the way they are. I have a good job, people who love and care about me, and a gorgeous dog who cuddles me and loves me unconditionally.'

They sat there, looking at each other for a long moment, lost in so many of the unspoken conversations they should have had over the years but never had.

Virgil was the first to look away, straightening the cutlery on the table and making way for their waiter to place their meals in front of them. The wine was poured and they began to eat, both clearly happy to have something else to focus on.

'I tried to call you,' he stated after a few minutes.

Clara swallowed her mouthful. 'What? When?'

She went to pull her smartphone from her pocket but he stopped her.

'Not tonight. I meant I tried to call you several months after I'd been in Montreal. You were right. That's what I was ringing to tell you. I wanted to tell you that you'd been right—that I'd ended up burning the candle at both ends, that I was overworked, exhausted and running myself ragged. I had no balance in my life any more and I realised, belatedly, that you were the person who had always provided me with that balance. Throughout medical school, during our internships… You were the one, Clara.'

He put down his fork and picked up his wine glass, taking a sip.

'I called you because I wanted to apologise, to tell you how incredibly sorry I was for the way I'd treated you and to ask if there was any possibility of us starting over.'

'Virgil.' She shook her head slowly. 'I didn't receive any calls from you.'

'When I called the phone service said the number was no longer valid. I tried emailing you. Still no response. I wrote to you but never received any reply.'

'Wait. You emailed me? Which email address? Where did you send the letter? I never received anything.'

Virgil stared at her for a long moment, his mind processing her words before he leaned his head back and slowly exhaled, unable to believe the weight which had just been lifted off his heart. She hadn't been ignoring him. She hadn't received his emails, hadn't received his letters— all of them begging her for another chance. A ray of hope sprang to life as he realised she hadn't rejected him at all.

'You didn't receive anything?' He slowly repeated her words.

'I was in hospital for months, and when I was discharged from the rehabilitation centre I moved in with my parents. Those first few months, Arthur took care of all my day-to-day issues, like paying bills, cancelling rental agreements, sorting things out with the hospital.'

'And you didn't receive anything from me?'

When she shook her head in confirmation he couldn't help but smile. It was short-lived.

'Wait.' He held up one hand. 'That means you never knew how sorry I was for the horrible way I'd treated you.' He shook his head sadly. 'My behaviour was arrogant, thoughtless and downright rude, and I'm *so* sorry, Clara. You deserved better.'

This news also made him realise why she wasn't willing to give him a chance now.

'I always thought you didn't reply as a way of telling me it was over. You were giving me the brush-off, letting me know that I'd blown it once and for all, and that there was no chance of a reconciliation.'

Hope continued to increase within him.

'Oh? So you thought that as you'd rejected me it was my turn to reject you?' Clearly he didn't know her at all. 'You thought I was that petty and wouldn't give you another chance?'

'I didn't say that.' He picked up his fork and started to eat his dinner again. 'But now that you know the truth—that I did try and apologise—does it make you want to change your mind about giving me another chance now?'

Her fork clattered to her plate as she stared at him in astonishment. 'Weren't you listening before?'

'I was listening,' he returned after finishing his mouthful. 'I heard everything you said. But it doesn't mean I'm going to stop hoping.'

'Hoping that there might be something other than professional friendship between us?' Clara shook her head. 'Stop hoping, Virgil, and just accept that this is the way it's going to be from now on.'

'But *why*?'

He needed to know. He felt certain there was something she wasn't telling him. But if he pressed her too much right now, she might stand up and walk out of the restaurant. He wanted to get things sorted out between them—to know exactly where he stood. He knew her of old, and he couldn't shake the sense that she wasn't telling him everything.

Clara put her knife and fork together on her plate, indicating she was done with her meal even though there was still half of it left.

'I think I should leave.'

'No. Wait. Clara, please stay.'

'Why?'

'Because...' He racked his brain, trying to think of a good reason. 'Because I want to tell you about my daughter. I have a phone full of pictures.'

She shook her head. 'I don't want to see them. Professional friends, Virgil.'

'Does Cedric have children?'

Clara frowned at the mention of the obstetrician at the Specialist Centre. 'Yes.'

'Have you seen pictures of them? Met them?'

'They've come to the Specialist Centre on occasion, yes.'

'So you've met them.'

'Yes.'

'What about Jane? Your receptionist? Does *she* have children?'

Sighing with impatience, she held up her hand. 'Yes, Jane has children. Yes, I've met them.'

'Then why, purely from a professional friendship point of view, can't you stay to let me be the proud, boasting daddy and show you some pictures of my Rosie?'

There was a hint of hurt in his tone and she knew she'd capitulate—but only because he'd made a valid point.

'OK. Fine.' She held out her hand. 'Give me your smartphone.'

Looking at pictures of an old boyfriend's child with another woman wasn't her idea of a fun evening, but with Virgil working at the Specialist Centre and hospital, there was every chance that Clara would eventually meet his daughter. Best to get the initial pain of accepting he'd had a child with someone else over and done with now.

Grinning, he was quick to find the pictures of his little girl and pass his phone to her.

'That first one was taken today. She's a cheeky thing.'

Clara stared at the photograph of the little girl with blonde hair, her eyes as perfectly blue as her father's. 'She's gorgeous, Virgil. How old did you say she was?'

'Three. My cheeky three-year-old. It doesn't end with the terrible twos!' He chuckled at his own joke and she nodded.

'Arthur has twin girls, only eighteen months old, and they get into so much mischief.' She continued to scroll through the photos on his phone. 'So I take it your wife was blonde?' The words were out before she could stop them and she quickly handed Virgil back his phone. 'Sorry. It's none of my business.'

'But it is, Clara—or at least I want it to be.'

'Virgil, we're just professional—'

'Diana. That was her name. She was French-Canadian and she reminded me a lot of you.'

'Really? Except that I'm very much Australian and have dark hair,' she felt compelled to point out.

She wanted to hear what Virgil had to say about the woman he'd married, but by the same token she didn't want to know anything. Knowing more about Virgil's life during the past six years would only make her more intrigued by him, and that was the last thing she wanted. Her life was great the way it was—wasn't it?

'Personality-wise, I mean. She liked old movies, like you. She liked the same authors you did. She loved to sing off-key in the shower and was always late for appointments.' He smiled sadly.

'Were you happy with her?' Again the question seemed to spring from her lips without thought.

'In the beginning, yes.' Virgil took a sip of his wine. 'After I didn't hear back from you I was—depressed.

Lonely. Diana was a nurse, and we became friends. She helped me to heal a broken heart.' Another sip of his wine. 'Our wedding was a pure impulse at the end of a clinical convention in Las Vegas. Tacky, I know, but it happens.'

'Chapel of Love?' she asked, trying to keep her emotional distance from what he was saying by injecting some humour.

'Something like that. Anyway, we decided to try and make a go of it.' He put his glass down and leaned forward. 'I thought there was no hope of reconciling with you, Clara. I had to move on with my life, try and find some new form of "normal".'

'Just like I had to move on with *my* life—to heal from my accident and travel overseas in order to find my new life.' She nodded, her words soft. 'I *do* understand, Virgil.'

When he reached for her hand she let him take it, linking their fingers together. When he gazed into her eyes she didn't look away, but instead saw the sincerity of his convictions. Perhaps she'd judged him too harshly. Perhaps he *had* changed. But if he truly had, did that mean she should give him another chance?

Her heart was screaming *yes*, but her mind... Her mind was definitely not saying no, and that was a scary prospect to consider. *Was* there a future for herself and Virgil just waiting to be explored? *Should* she take the chance? She honestly didn't know.

CHAPTER FOUR

WHEN CLARA ARRIVED home from her dinner with Virgil she sent her brother a text message to check if he was free to talk. A moment later her phone rang.

'Hey, sis.'

'You busy?'

'Nope. Just waiting up for my wife to get home from her long shift at the hospital. The wine is chilling and I'm about to draw her a long and relaxing bubble bath.'

'And the girls?'

'Sound asleep—at the moment.' Arthur chuckled. 'But tonight Daddy's on duty and Mummy gets to relax.'

Clara sighed. 'See? Why can't I find a guy like you?'

She sat down on the lounge and a moment later, her dog, Fuzzy-Juzzy, jumped up beside her, expecting to be patted. Clara didn't disappoint the dog.

'You're all about the caring and the listening and the supportive attitude.'

Arthur chuckled. 'I know. I'm quite a catch—as I remind Maybelle on a semi-regular basis. Anyway, little sis, what's up?'

'Why would anything be up?'

'Because you don't usually call me this late at night, sounding so serious.'

'Uh—well—I had dinner with Virgil tonight.'

There was a momentary silence on the other end of the line, and for a second she thought her brother had hung up.

'Arthur?'

'I'm here. I just didn't think you were going to have anything to do with him—apart from being professional, I mean. At least that's what you told me before he arrived back in town.'

The protective note in Arthur's tone was unmistakable.

'It wasn't a romantic dinner.'

She tried to block out the mental vision of them sitting at that table for two, fingers linked, staring into each other's eyes. What had she been *thinking*? That was the problem. She hadn't been thinking. All she'd been feeling at that moment when she'd let him link his hand with hers, was that she'd missed him. Even though she'd been through therapy, even though she'd tried new things, met new people, done everything and anything she could in order to pull her life back together, at the end of the day the simple and honest fact was that she'd missed him.

Of course there was no way she could say that to Arthur, or else he'd don his protective big brother superhero cape and stand guard over her as he'd done in the past. She didn't need him to do that any more. She was more than capable of donning her own superhero cape.

Clara cleared her throat. 'We—ah—we simply needed to set out some ground rules so we know where each other stands.'

'And where *does* the almighty Virgil Arterton stand? Still on his pedestal? With a pole stuck up his—?'

'Actually, he was very apologetic.'

Arthur snorted. 'I'll bet he was.'

'Arthur...' She hesitated for a moment, unsure how to ask what she needed to ask. 'Virgil mentioned that several months after he'd been in Montreal, he tried to contact me again. Do you know anything about that?'

'No!' The surprise in Arthur's tone was clear.

'He said he tried to call but the number was disconnected.'

'He would have tried your old number at your old apartment.'

'He also said that he tried to email me and even wrote me a letter.'

'He did?'

'You seriously don't know anything about this?

'I don't. I really don't. Back when you were in hospital I cancelled your phone, your internet connection and your lease. I had your mail redirected to Mum and Dad's house for six months. I figured six months was enough time to change over any details. With regard to your emails, I think the only email address you had at the time was the one at Melbourne General, and that was shut down when you stopped working there.'

She continued to stroke Juzzy as she mulled over what her brother was saying. 'So you and Mum and Dad weren't protecting me from Virgil?'

'Honestly, Clara, if an email or a letter from Virgil had found its way to me, I would have given it to you. I would have discussed the possible emotional outcome with Mum and Dad, and probably your doctors, before giving it to you, but I would never have kept it from you. Neither would Mum or Dad. We love you, yes. We want to protect you, yes, but we wouldn't have hidden something like that from you.'

'That's what I thought. I just needed to check—just needed to be sure.'

Her phone had been disconnected, her email address had been wiped from the hospital server and her mail redirection had probably expired by the time Virgil had tried to get in touch.

'OK.' She heaved a heavy sigh. 'Thanks.'

'Are you OK? You don't want to talk about things some more? You could come down and join us for a drink. Maybelle won't mind. She loves seeing you and—'

Clara smiled. 'I'm OK, Arthur. Humpty Dumpty *has* been put back together again, remember?'

'I know, but I'm always going to worry about you—and especially where Virgil Arterton is concerned.'

Clara felt the warmth of his brotherly love. 'I'm fine,' she reiterated, before signing off with their usual farewell. 'Love you, bro.'

'Love you, too, sis.'

Clara disconnected the call and looked down at Fuzzy-Juzzy.

'Virgil tried to contact me, to apologise and ask for a second chance. What do you make of that, Juzzy?'

The dog's answer was to snuggle in closer.

'All these years and now he's back. I guess it's time for me to start walking through the next chapter of my life. The chapter where Virgil and I are nothing more than professional friends, consulting about patients together and being polite.'

So why couldn't she stop thinking about the way he'd held her hand, the way he'd looked into her eyes? She'd seen his hope that they'd be able to patch up the past and move forward into a happier future. He was wearing his heart on his sleeve and that was yet another indication that he'd changed.

'I just need to walk very carefully,' she told her dog. 'Very carefully indeed.'

During the week following their dinner—Virgil's first week working at the Specialist Centre as well as at Victory Hospital—Clara was surprised at how little she actually saw him. Twice she'd seen him walking through the corridors of the Specialist Centre, but both times he'd been deep in conversation with Cedric. The two men had nodded politely, acknowledging her, before continuing to discuss a patient they shared.

Perhaps this could work after all. Virgil had listened, and was clearly being the professional friend she'd asked him to be.

So why did the knowledge make her feel forlorn, as though she was missing out on something really special?

She shook the thought away and went back to work.

On the weekend she was rostered for an evening shift in the ED, and as Virgil didn't hold any clinics at the weekend, there was no real chance of her running into him.

'And even if he *is* at the hospital he'll probably be up on the surgical wards, doing a quick check on his patients before going home to spend time with his daughter,' she told Juzzy. 'Nothing to worry about.'

Clara finished pinning her hair into a bun at the nape of her neck.

'He has his professional life, I have mine, and that's that. No reason to feel forlorn. No reason to think I'm missing out on something great. I'm happy with my life the way it is.'

She nuzzled closer to the fluffy Pomeranian, receiving a lick on her cheek in return.

'I love you, too, Juzzy,' she told the dog.

After putting Juzzy to bed, Clara headed out of the apartment and drove to the hospital.

Her shift turned out to be an average one for a Saturday night. Kids with coughs, teenagers who had been drinking too much and a few patients with broken bones.

An hour before her shift was due to end, early Sunday morning, Larissa, one of the ED nurses, beckoned her over to the nurses' station.

'Just received a call from the paramedics. They're on

their way in with Michelle DeCosta, who's been complaining of—'

'Abdominal pains,' Clara finished for her, and nodded. 'Michelle's one of my patients. I saw her in the clinic last week and made an appointment for her to see Dr Arterton as soon as possible. Virgil was able to squeeze her in yesterday, but apparently she didn't show. I was going to follow-up her no-show on Monday.'

'Clearly the pains have become more intense. Do you want me to call Dr Arterton in for the consult?'

'Let's order some tests first—see what we're dealing with.'

Clara didn't want to bother Virgil.

She turned and headed towards a treatment room, wanting to ensure it was ready for Michelle's impending arrival, but after a few steps she stopped and sighed.

Michelle suffered from acute anxiety. Even when Clara had told her patient she was referring her to Virgil, Michelle had had a minor panic attack. Clara had managed to calm the woman down, telling her that Virgil was an exceptional surgeon, that he would take good care of her and that Victory Hospital was fortunate he'd come to operate there. She didn't want Michelle having another anxiety attack now.

Clara turned back to Larissa. 'On second thoughts, call Virgil in now. When Michelle gets here I'll order an abdominal ultrasound and see if my suspicions are confirmed.'

'What do you think it is?'

'Gallstones.'

'I'll call him in right away.' Larissa picked up the phone.

When the ambulance arrived Clara was waiting for Michelle, ready to care for her patient. As the paramedics wheeled Michelle's stretcher into the hospital, Clara realised Michelle was slap-bang in the middle of a panic attack.

'She's refused all medication,' Adrian, Michelle's husband, told her. 'She doesn't want to take anything—either for the pain or to help calm her nerves.'

He was clearly worried about his wife, trying to hold her hand as the stretcher was taken through to the treatment room.

'I know she doesn't have any allergies so I'll draw up some Methoxyflurane—which should help calm her down long enough to get some tests done.'

Clara headed over to Michelle, eager to calm the woman down.

'Clara. Clara! I'm so happy you're here. Why *are* you here? This is the hospital. I'm sorry I didn't see Dr Arterton.' Michelle spoke fast, her words tumbling out in a rush. 'I was too scared. I was—I was shaking and unable to move. Adrian tried to get me to go but I was scared, Clara. I was *so* scared.'

Even now Michelle was shaking. She was white, her breathing was rapid, and even if Clara had wanted to check the other woman's blood pressure there was no way she'd be able to get a cuff onto her arm.

'It's OK, Michelle.' Clara hooked up the oxygen and held the mask out to Michelle. 'Nice deep breaths. You can do it.'

'You're not angry?' Michelle checked, accepting the mask from Clara.

'Of course not. What I *am* concerned about is the pain you're in.' Clara spoke in soothing tones, placing her hand on the woman's shoulder in a show of support. 'I'm here, and I'm not going to leave you until we know exactly what's causing the pain and how it's going to be treated. OK? Now, I want you to try and focus on your breathing. Slow it down. In and out.'

Her words were calming, yet firm. She needed Michelle to focus and thankfully, as Michelle held her gaze, the two of them practised breathing in slowly and then exhaling slowly.

Once her breathing was more steady, the nursing staff were able to take Michelle's vitals and Clara was able to give the injection of Methoxyflurane, which would not only help to keep Michelle calm, but also assist with the abdominal pain.

By the time Virgil arrived she had the results of Michelle's abdominal ultrasound, which confirmed her diagnosis of gallstones.

'Clara! What are you doing here?' he asked when he saw her standing at the nurses' station.

His tone had resonated with a hint of delight at seeing her so unexpectedly and he'd smiled. Darn it—*why* had he smiled? She hated it when he smiled, because when he did it caused the butterflies in her stomach to churn with excitement. She didn't want to be aware of his nearness, his scent, of the way he held his body so perfectly that his polo shirt pulled across his broad shoulders. She didn't want to be this attracted to him.

'It's my bi-monthly shift in Emergency at the hospital.'

She didn't want to dwell on anything but the main reason why *he* was here. She didn't want chit-chat—she just wanted to focus on getting Michelle sorted out. She handed him Michelle's file and began discussing the case.

Virgil read the results of the scans and tests Clara had ordered. 'She has anxiety?'

'I've been treating her for the past two years. She's actually much better than previously, but coming to hospital and being out of her comfort zone has triggered her anxiety.'

'Of course.' He held Michelle's notes in his hand. 'As you're Michelle's GP, I think it might be best if you come with me when I go and talk to her. That way she'll have your reassuring presence to fall back on when she learns she'll need to have surgery.'

Clara nodded, pleased he was thinking about the emotional welfare of their patient rather than playing the part of brisk, arrogant surgeon.

As they headed to Michelle's room, he asked, 'Have you told her the diagnosis?'

'I've told her she has gallstones and that she may need surgery.'

'How did she react to that news?'

'She started to hyperventilate. But it didn't last too long and she was able to control her breathing. Last time I checked, she was sleeping.'

He sighed. 'Unfortunately, we're going to need to wake her.'

Together they woke Michelle, who was far more relaxed now than when she'd arrived. Her husband Adrian sat in the corner.

'Hello, Michelle. I'm Virgil Arterton, the new general surgeon here at Victory Hospital. It appears, as I'm sure you've been told, that you have gallstones.'

Michelle nodded, tears springing to her eyes. 'I'm sorry I didn't have the scan sooner. I'm sorry to be causing all this trouble. And I'm sorr—'

'It's perfectly all right,' Virgil interrupted, putting his hand on hers and instantly soothing his patient. 'One of the gallstones is quite large, measuring in at almost one centimetre. The other isn't quite as big, but both will need to be removed.'

'H-how?' The worry in Michelle's voice was prominent.

'It'll be a short procedure in which I'll remove your gallbladder. It's all done in the day surgery unit, so you'll be able to go home the same day.'

'What?' Michelle's eyes widened at this information.

'The same day? But what if I have problems—what if the pain comes back and—?'

Her breathing started to accelerate again and she reached blindly for her husband's hand. Adrian was instantly on his feet, taking her hand in his and trying to soothe her.

'Would you prefer to say in overnight?' Clara asked. 'That way we can keep you under observation for twenty-four hours after the operation. And once you're home we can put you on the district nursing roster. I can also come and do a house-call to check on you,' she offered.

She glanced at Virgil and the unspoken communication they'd used to share, seemed to kick in. With one look she was able to convey to him that whilst Michelle indeed only required a small operation, it was her anxiety which was the bigger threat.

'That sounds like an excellent solution, Dr Lewis.' He nodded in Clara's direction before addressing his comments to Michelle. 'I'll admit you to the ward now, and then I can organise a theatre for later this afternoon. All being well, you can go home tomorrow.' He smiled at his patient, his tone reassuring.

Michelle looked from Clara to Virgil and then to Adrian, who nodded encouragingly. 'Uh… OK…'

'You're not alone, Michelle. We're here to look after you,' Clara reassured her, before she and Virgil headed back to the nurses' station.

Throughout the consult Clara had been aware of Virgil's every move, and she had to admit that his bedside manner was exemplary. Was he trying to show her how much he had changed? If so, it was working—because she *was* noticing. It seemed the chauvinistic, arrogant man he'd been all those years ago had been replaced by someone who was calm, caring and absolutely charming. He clearly didn't see his patients as just a number on a file, but rather as the individuals they were.

They left Michelle in the care of the nurses who were organising her transfer to the ward, while Clara helped Virgil with the necessary paperwork to book an operating theatre for later that day and contact the anaesthetist.

'Where would I be without you?' he crooned as he leaned back in the chair and flexed his arms above his head.

The action caused the polo shirt he was wearing to pull tightly across his upper arms and chest, and Clara found it difficult to look away. Clearly, he'd kept in shape. When she finally raised her gaze to meet his, it was to find him regarding her with an interested smile.

'Like what you see?' he teased.

Clara felt an instant heat come to her cheeks as he flexed his muscles in the familiar pose body builders used. Although it was early Sunday morning in the ED, there were still quite a few of the night staff around to witness him teasing her.

'Behave,' she warned him, looking away and straightening some papers on the desk.

She needed to be doing something other than looking at the way that shirt fitted him to perfection. She had so many memories of him teasing her this way, of joking together, of laughing and enjoying themselves, and until that moment she hadn't realised how much she'd missed that easy camaraderie they'd shared. She'd missed him. Missed his friendship, missed his calming manner, missed the way he would stare into her eyes and make her feel as though she were the most important person in the world to him.

Clara glanced at him over her shoulder, only to discover he was watching her intently, the smile still in place.

'Do I really need to behave?'

'Yes.'

'Why?' He glanced around. 'No one's looking—and, besides, it used to be *me* who was always telling *you* to behave.'

'Untrue,' she declared instantly.

'*You* were the one who had the idea to put sticky tape over all the taps in our lab at medical school. *You* were the one with the party trick of drinking a whole glass of water whilst doing a handstand. And I distinctly remember several of us turning up to ward round wearing cartoon masks.'

'OK. OK.' She couldn't help but smile at the memories he was recounting.

Virgil pointed at her. 'Another one of your brilliant ideas.'

He chuckled, the warm sound washing over her.

'And *I* was the one who took the blame for them all—well, for the sticking tape over the taps, at least.'

'The cartoon masks were when we were doing a rotation in Paediatrics. The kids loved them,' she felt compelled to point out.

Virgil stood and looked down into her upturned face. 'We used to have so much fun together, Clara.'

'We did, but we're not medical students any more.'

He rolled his eyes. 'Tell me about it. I found another grey hair yesterday—on my chest!'

Clara couldn't help but laugh at the disgusted look on his face. 'Oh, Virgil. We have so many wonderful shared memories.'

'We do.' He placed one hand on her shoulder. 'Which is why I really want to be more than just nodding-in-the-corridor professional friends with you.'

'But you're wanting something I can't give.'

'All I want is a second chance—and you can give me that. A chance to be your friend again. A *real* friend, not just an acquaintance.'

'Friends?' She mulled it over. A large part of her wanted so desperately to say yes, but she needed to protect her heart. 'It's not as easy as that.'

'Yes, it is.'

She closed her eyes for a moment before meeting his gaze. 'You broke my heart. You really broke it, Virgil. So much pain...' Tears welled in her eyes.

He shook his head. 'It wasn't me...it wasn't the *real* me. My mind was overtaken by my own stupidity, my own arrogance, my own self-importance and I hurt you. But I've worked on those negative qualities, Clara. I'm a wiser, more well-rounded person nowadays. Please?'

His words had been soft and intimate, yet imploring. She could see the sincerity in his eyes and she knew she was about to capitulate—against her better judgement.

'OK.'

'OK? OK, you'll give me a second chance?'

'To be my *friend*.'

'Yeah. *Yeah.* That's good. That's excellent.'

And before she knew what he was about he'd drawn her close and hugged her.

'Thank you. You won't regret it.'

'I'd better not,' she mumbled against his chest, doing her best not become hypnotised by his alluring scent.

Although he'd surprised her with the hug, the warmth from his body meshed with hers and she closed her eyes, savouring every second to think about later.

'Now, let me go, you big oaf, before someone sees us.'

'And what if they do?' He released his hold on her and shrugged one shoulder. 'We're just two old friends enjoying a quick hug. Nothing wrong with that.'

'Hmm...' She frowned at him and couldn't help but laugh. She hoped it was true—that her old friend was back—because she had missed him. She'd missed the good times, the sad times and the quiet times.

'And my first act of friendship is to ask you over to my house for dinner next weekend.'

'Virgil, take it easy.'

He held up his hands to ward off her words. 'I know. You think I'm rushing things.'

'A bit, yeah.'

'But I really want you to meet Rosie. She's my world, Clara, and I want to share that with you. Oh, and you can meet my housekeeper, Gwenda. She's nice, too.'

'Will you be cooking?'

'No.'

'Good. You were always really bad.'

'Then you'll be pleased to know I've improved.'

He seemed to be filled with energy, his eyes alive with excitement at the thought of her coming to dinner at his house and meeting his daughter.

'But Gwenda will be cooking. I have a clinic at the Specialist Centre on Saturday morning and I promised Rosie we'd go to the park in the afternoon.' He angled his head to the side and raised an eyebrow. 'You could come to the park if you'd like? Then we could go back to my house for dinner.'

'Let's just take it one small step at a time. Besides, I have house calls.'

'Right.' He nodded. 'And Michelle will probably be on that list, won't she?' he stated.

'More than likely.'

'Good.' He paused, his stance changing from her cheeky friend, to the serious surgeon. 'It's *good* that anxiety disorders are now more widely accepted by practitioners as well as the community at large.'

'Hear, hear.'

'Actually, would you like to be there for her surgery? I'm sure if she saw you in the ante-chamber of the surgical suite she'd be more comfortable. She has a lot of confidence in you, Clara.'

'You sound surprised.'

'No. I'm not at all surprised that you're a great GP—that you not only care about your patients but they care about you in return and value your opinions. You made the right decision about your career and I'm glad it's worked out for you.'

'Really?'

'Yes. When I'm wrong, I say I'm wrong—and I was wrong.'

Clara clutched her hands to her chest as she looked up at him. 'Thank you, Virgil. That means a lot.'

'So... Michelle's surgery? Think you'll be able to make it?'

As she pondered coming back to the hospital this afternoon to see Michelle, after doing a full night in the ED, she began to realise how tired she was. Still, it wasn't every day she received an invitation to watch a surgical procedure—even if it was just the removal of a gallbladder.

'Yes. I'll be there. You're right. It will help Michelle.'

'You really are a kind and caring doctor, Clara. I'm proud of you.'

As he headed off to do whatever it was he needed to do, and as Clara finished her shift and headed home to get some sleep, she couldn't believe how wonderful it felt—not only to have her friend Virgil back in her life—but to hear that he was proud of her. That meant a lot.

CHAPTER FIVE

WHY AM I happy that I have his approval? That he's proud of me? It's not like I need his approval to be content with my life. I'm already content...so why does it matter?

Did she still care what Virgil thought of her? *Did* she still care that much about his opinions? She had in the past—until he'd changed from Dr Jekyll to Mr Hyde.

She opened the door to her apartment, greeted instantly by Fuzzy-Juzzy.

'Oh, hello, darling. Hello!' She picked up the dog and cuddled her close before letting the fuzzy Pomeranian go. 'Yes. It's breakfast time. Were you a good girl, sleeping all night in your bed or did you sleep on my bed?'

Clara put her bag and keys down, then checked her bedroom. Sure enough, there was a little round spot in the middle of her bed where her dog had slept. At the end of the bed was a step stool, so that Juzzy could get up and down from Clara's bed. When Clara really didn't want the dog to disturb her sleep, she would move the stool away, but on nights when she was at the hospital she left it there, pleased that the dog missed her enough to curl up on her bed. It made her feel loved.

There was a knock at her door and she quickly went to answer it. Juzzy was equally excited.

Clara was pleased to find her sister-in-law on the other side.

'Morning!' Maybelle said, and gave Clara a hug. 'We're just about to take the girls and the dogs for a walk. Shall we take Juzzy for you so you can get some sleep?'

'Oh…that would be wonderful.' Clara sighed and went to get Juzzy's leash. 'I *love* having family living in the same building.'

'How was your shift?' Maybelle asked as Clara tried to clip the leash to a very excited Juzzy.

'Good.'

As she said the word Clara couldn't help but smile as memories of Virgil teasing her, Virgil laughing with her, Virgil being absolutely delighted she was giving him a second chance, flashed through her mind.

'Wait. What was *that*?' Maybelle queried.

'What? What was what?'

'You were doing that little half-smile—that smile you do when you're secretly excited about something.'

'No, I wasn't.'

'Yeah, you were.' Maybelle nodded, then gasped as realisation dawned. 'Was *Virgil* at the hospital?' she asked.

'Yes. I had a patient with gallstones. He was called in for a consult.' Clara waved her words away as though it had all been nothing but completely professional.

'But—*Virgil*. I've seen him around the hospital, Clara. He's gorgeous.' At Clara's raised eyebrows, Maybelle continued. 'But definitely not my type. My type is my husband.'

Clara smiled at her friend. 'Yes, Virgil was there. Yes, we chatted. Yes, it was…nice.'

'Exciting! Are you going to give him another chance?' Maybelle asked.

'Another chance to break my heart?' Clara stared sceptically at her friend. 'No. A chance to be my friend again, yes. I mean, we're working together, and we have so much history, and we know each other so well—'

'And he's totally your type,' Maybelle added softly.

Clara sighed. 'He *was* my type of man, once upon a time.'

'Maybe he has really changed. People do. *I* did.'

'But you're you and you were forced to change—forced into a life you never really asked for until you were able to find your way back to total happiness.'

'Perhaps Virgil thought he *had* to change—that he had to impress all the other arrogant surgeons and be just like them in order to get ahead in the surgical world?'

Clara frowned. 'Hmm… I never thought of it like that before.'

'Granted, the way he treated you was horrible and heart-breaking, but what if he really has changed, Clara?'

She sighed again. 'If he has, then taking it very, *very* slowly is the only way to go. I might like laughing with him, being friends with him, but I don't know if I can ever trust him again.'

The door to the downstairs apartment closed and the noise level immediately rose as Arthur pushed the double pram, complete with chattering little girls, into the entryway. Their dogs barked with excitement and Juzzy joined in.

'It's a good decision to take things slow,' Maybelle said with a determined look as she took Juzzy's leash and allowed herself to be pulled away. 'I'm glad you've agreed to be friends. Now, eat breakfast and sleep. Doctor's orders.'

Clara closed the door and couldn't help but do a little dance. It was exciting to know Virgil was back to being her friend. 'And *just* your friend,' she warned herself aloud as she went to the kitchen.

As she ate some food, she reflected on how he'd smiled at her, and how she'd been moved by the sincerity of his expressions and impressed with his treatment of Michelle. He wasn't the same man she'd known during medical school, but he seemed to be a new and improved version, one with wisdom—and another grey hair on his chest.

She smiled at the thought as she brushed her teeth and fell into bed, pulling the covers around her and feeling just as happy and secure as she'd felt when being hugged in Virgil's arms.

'Virgil...' She sighed with contentment before drifting off to sleep.

Clara managed to return to the hospital in time for Michelle's gallbladder surgery, and saw her patient relaxing when she realised Clara would be present.

'Thank you. *Both* of you,' Michelle said, looking at Clara and then Virgil before closing her eyes and allowing the anaesthetist to do his job.

The surgery was completed without complications, and as Michelle was taken through to recovery, Virgil wrote up the notes.

'How was that?' he asked as he added his signature and closed the notes.

'Watching keyhole surgery?' Clara gave him two thumbs up. 'A perfectly fun way to spend an afternoon.'

Virgil laughed at her antics and Clara grinned. It was so nice to feel as though she had her friend back. 'Thanks again for letting me be here. I know it made a difference to Michelle.'

'You may be surprised by this, Clara, but there are quite a lot of surgeons who aren't just scalpel-happy jerks. Sure, there are the arrogant holier-than-thou types, and for a while I felt I had to be one of them in order to impress them, but at the end of the day I do what I do in order to help people. There are plenty of us who actually care about our patients.'

'Huh. I *am* surprised. But I'm glad you're one of them.'

As they exited the theatre, heading to the change rooms, she was highly aware of her *friend* walking beside her. Highly aware that he was incredibly tall and somehow looked incredibly sexy in theatre scrubs. Highly aware of the way his hand almost brushed hers. Highly aware of that subtle spicy scent he wore. She didn't want to be—she wanted to view him as she had in medical school, as her very good-looking friend who was there to support her, to have fun and to laugh with her.

Upon reaching the changing room doors, he paused. 'Listen, are you free to grab a cup of coffee in the cafeteria before heading home?'

She smiled up at him as she put in the code for the female changing rooms. Opening the door, she shook her head. 'I've got so many household chores to do before tomorrow morning, the most important of which is washing my clothes so I have something to wear to work in the morning.' She tilted her head to the side. 'Not *all* of us employ housekeepers, you know.'

'It's only because I have a child who can't be left alone,' he defended quickly, but grinned at her as he put in the code for the male changing rooms. 'OK. I guess I'll see you around the Specialist Centre and—' he proffered as he opened the door '—hopefully wearing clean clothes.'

He winked at her, his teasing tone rushing over her with delight.

Entering the changing rooms, she walked to the bench and sat down because her knees were starting to wobble. *Friends.* They were friends. Friends *only* and at her insistence. It was great to know that Virgil wanted more—that he wanted to give their relationship another go and that he had visions of spending the rest of his life with her—but that was far too much for her to compute and accept right now.

He was back in her life. She'd accepted that. They were giving their friendship another go. She'd accepted that too. And although she was attracted to him—although she was being driven insane by his scent and her heart rate increased whenever he winked or smiled or laughed with her—that didn't mean she had to rush headlong into a full reunion with him.

'He hurt you. He hurt you badly,' she whispered to herself, needing to find logic and common sense in her crazy new world. 'You've been friends before and you can be friends again. Nothing more.'

With that, she drew in a deep, cleansing breath and stood up, heading to her locker so she could get changed and head home. She sniffed the clothes she'd worn to the hospital and screwed up her nose. Yep. Definitely time to do the laundry.

For some reason the thought of not looking her best, the thought of not smelling like a sweet-scented rose, especially when she was around Virgil, made her feel highly self-conscious.

It's not for Virgil, she told herself as she drove home. *It's for yourself. Dress for yourself. Wear your hair the way you want to.*

And if Virgil found her irresistibly attractive, then so be it.

Monday and Tuesday were both hectic days, and Clara was glad when she arrived home that she could eat dinner then fall into bed, resting and relaxing with Juzzy by her side.

On Wednesday, she had a patient cancel just before lunch.

'You can take a whole forty minutes,' Jane told her.

'It's sad that that's the most exciting thing to happen to me all week,' Clara said as she grabbed her wallet and headed out through the door.

Around the Specialist Centre and the hospital were several cafés and novelty shops, as well as two florists. She'd just stepped outside the centre when someone called her name. She turned to see Virgil heading her way.

'Where are you off to?' he asked.

'A patient cancelled and I have forty minutes for lunch.'

'Whoa! Pure luxury,' he exaggerated as he fell into step beside her. 'Mind some company?'

'Sure. Who did you have in mind?'

He groaned at her lame joke. 'You're *funny*. Hey, how's Michelle doing?'

'Really great. Once she arrived home her anxiety settled down and she's letting her husband pamper her. I *have* sent you a professional progress report with words to that effect.'

'Good to hear. So, what do you feel like for lunch? Salad? Burger and fries? Chicken roll?'

'Ice-cream and fudge,' she stated, and pointed to Marni's café, which was next to one of the florists.

'Ice-cream for lunch? I should have guessed. After all, I do remember you eating a whole litre of fudge ripple when studying for exams.'

'I like ice-cream. It's not a crime.'

'No, it is not.' He held the door to Marni's café open and together they went in. 'I've never had anything mixed in with my ice-cream before.'

'You do *not* know what you're missing out on, buddy. You're going to love it.'

'I don't know… I don't mind having things on the side, but mixed in?' Virgil frowned and shook his head.

'Go on. Live life on the edge.' She chuckled before perusing the selection of ice-creams.

'Yeah. I need to do more crazy things in my life. OK. You've talked me into it.'

It was nice. Nice to be around Clara, nice to hear her

laugh, nice to tease her, and incredible to see her smiling—not only smiling but smiling at *him*.

When he'd seen her in Melbourne at the retrieval examinations, he'd really had second thoughts about moving back to Loggeen, but now, being with her, sitting opposite her whilst eating ice-cream and enjoying an easy camaraderie, warmed his heart.

Perhaps there was a chance that he could win her back. Although he'd blurted out his true intentions when they'd had dinner, and had thought such a declaration would send her running for the hills, here he was, sitting with her, eating ice-cream with bits of fudge mixed through it.

After Diana's death, when he'd been left alone to raise their daughter, he'd gone to therapy, needing to find some semblance of meaning to his life. Yes, his work made him happy. Yes, he loved spending time with his little girl. But even with Diana, there had always been one aspect of true happiness which had been missing, and he'd realised, belatedly, that Clara was that one aspect.

He was content with his life—just as she'd told him she was content with hers—however, there was more to life than simply being content. What about being incredibly happy? What about finding that one person who was your other half? Spending time with them, sharing the ups and downs with them, growing old together with them?

Through his therapy sessions he'd come to realise that the only time in his life he'd been truly happy was when he'd been with Clara. It wasn't that he'd relied on her for his own happiness, but rather that being with her had enhanced his joy.

Although Diana had helped him through a difficult time in his life, they hadn't had the solid foundation of friendship he'd needed in which to succeed at marriage. If Diana hadn't passed away, he knew their marriage would have required a lot of work. Even then, there would have been no guarantee that it wouldn't have ended in divorce. That hadn't been an easy realisation for him to deal with, but slowly he'd come to terms with it.

'Happiness isn't a myth,' his therapist had told him. 'But happiness *is* made up of a lot of small things—and being content with who you are as a person, is a big part of that. Finding someone who is content within themselves, someone you're compatible with, someone you just can't wait to share good or bad news with, knowing they'll be there for you no matter what, is the difficult part.'

And that was when Virgil had had his epiphany. He'd already found that one person, and he'd let her go. Diana's death had taught him something else as well—that life was too short not to go after what you really wanted, and *he* really wanted to spend the rest of his life with Clara.

'You're frowning at your ice-cream,' she pointed out as she finished her delicious confectionery.

'Huh?' He jerked his head up and looked at her. 'Sorry. Deep in thought.'

'Ooh. Deep thoughts are dangerous—which is why I don't mind the occasional brain-freeze. It helps me not to think too deeply.'

He chuckled at her words.

'You don't like the fudge mixed in, do you?' she asked.

Virgil slowly shook his head. 'I don't, but I know Rosie would. I'll have to bring her here to try it out.'

'At least you're not letting your own dislikes influence her. Let me know when you're bringing her here and I'll join you.'

'You will?' He was surprised at her words.

'Sure. I never pass up the opportunity to eat fudge and ice-cream.'

'All right, then.' He held out his hand and Clara shook it. 'It's a date.' He paused, still holding her hand, still needing that contact, still delighting in the softness of her skin. 'You *are* still coming to dinner this Saturday?'

'Yeah.'

She nodded and he released her hand, then watched as Clara eyed his half-finished ice-cream as it melted in the bowl.

'Are you going to finish that?'

Chuckling, he passed the bowl to her. 'Here you go, you ice-cream-a-holic.'

Wanting to finish his leftovers? This was good. This was *very* good.

Clara shifted her present for Virgil's daughter to her other hand and smoothed down her top. Ridiculous, she chided herself. Being so preoccupied with her appearance simply for Virgil. She'd told herself over and over that they were simply friends and nothing more, yet this was the fourth outfit she'd changed into before leaving home.

She'd stopped by the toy store yesterday, and after long minutes of deliberation had ended up buying an animated clock, which was guaranteed to lull any child to sleep at night and bring a giggle to their lips during the day. She hoped Rosie liked it.

Resisting the impulse to press the doorbell again, Clara fluffed her ankle-length skirt and smoothed her white top again. Where on earth *was* he? Didn't he realise she was nervous about meeting his daughter? If Rosie didn't like her then— Clara stopped. Then what? Why did it matter whether or not Virgil's daughter liked her? Sure, they'd managed to make it through a whole week being a bit more than professional acquaintances, and Clara had enjoyed every moment she'd spent with Virgil, but if his three-year-old daughter didn't take a shine to her, it wouldn't be the end of the world.

After a few more impatient moments, she heard footsteps heading towards the door. Exhaling a deep, calming breath, she pasted a smile in place.

'Clara Lewis?' The door was opened by a plump, elderly woman with short grey hair and green eyes.

'Yes.' Clara quickly responded.

'Come on in. Virgil won't be a moment. He's just putting away his toys.'

There was a slight smirk on the other woman's lips and Clara instantly warmed to her.

'*His* toys?' she queried as she came inside.

The woman closed the door behind them. 'He needs to set a good example for his daughter by removing his computer and paperwork from the dining room table.' She chuckled.

'OK...' Clara remarked, feeling a little unsure of the correct response.

The woman held out her hand. 'I'm Gwenda, by the way.' Gwenda glanced at the beautifully wrapped present and smiled. 'Rosie is going to love that wrapping paper.'

Clara nodded. 'I specifically chose shiny paper for that very reason. My nieces always love this kind of wrapping.'

'How old are they?' Gwenda asked as she led them through the house, Clara's flat shoes making a faint tapping sound on the polished wooden floor.

'Eighteen months old—they're twins.'

'Double the trouble, double the love!' Gwenda stated.

'And double the nappies, as my sister-in-law says.'

Clara followed Gwenda.

'Come through to the dining room. We'll be eating straight away, so Rosie can have her bath and go to bed.'

'Sounds good,' Clara agreed.

The large dining table was set at one end with four place settings—the fourth having a Mickey Mouse theme. Place-mat, fork, spoon and cup were all adorned with Disney characters. A booster seat was on the chair and Virgil, with his back to Clara, was seating his daughter comfortably.

When he stepped back, Clara was captivated by the little girl, with her blonde hair and the same perfect blue eyes as her father. She'd looked adorable in the pictures Virgil had shown her, but in person there was definitely a hint of mischief about her. At the moment, though, she was gazing lovingly up at her father, as though he'd hung the moon just for her.

'Thanks for coming, Clara,' Virgil stated, and it was only then that Clara glanced his way.

He was dressed casually in jeans and a cotton shirt. She looked back at his daughter, who had spied the present in Clara's hands.

'It's a present? A present for Rosie?'

Her blue eyes twinkled with delight, her little hands coming forward with anticipation. Best of all, her little voice held the hint of a French accent, and Clara realised the girl was most likely bilingual. Having been born in Montreal, it was little wonder.

'Uh—' Clara seemed to snap out of the fog which had surrounded her at seeing Virgil with his daughter. 'Yes. This is for you.'

'You shouldn't have. She's spoiled enough.' He watched as his daughter took the present, prompting, 'Manners, Rosie?'

'Merci,' Rosie replied dutifully, her little hands trying to find the join in the paper where the sticky tape was located.

As the little girl unwrapped the gift, Virgil edged a little closer to Clara.

'You look lovely,' he said quietly.

Clara turned her head. 'Thank you.' She allowed her gaze to flit fleetingly over his lithe frame. 'You don't look so bad yourself.'

'Why, thank you, Dr Lewis.'

'You're welcome, Dr Arterton.'

They stared into each other's eyes for a long moment, and then the smiles started to slip, their easy, joking manner being replaced by one of tantalising awareness. He looked good. He smelled good. He was looking at her lips—and she was looking at his.

As though both realising the danger they might find themselves in, they looked away, focusing on the little girl, who had managed to get the ribbon off and was scrunching the shiny gold paper.

'Would you like some help, blossom?' Virgil carefully removed the sticky tape and helped her to open the box. 'Hey. What's in here?'

As Virgil helped Rosie to remove the clock, Clara took the opportunity to put her attraction to Virgil out of her mind. She was here to meet his daughter, not to ogle him in front of the child.

'Wow!' Rosie exclaimed. 'Cow. Dog. Cat. Spoon.'

'It's "Hey Diddle Diddle",' Virgil told her. Rosie reached for the clock and her father quickly said, 'Gently, blossom. Touch lightly.'

The clock, shaped like a moon, had three-dimensional characters from the nursery rhyme around it.

'It plays two different tunes,' Clara volunteered. 'One for bedtime and one for daytime.' She'd put a battery in and set the clock to the correct time before wrapping it.

Virgil sat it on the table, out of reach of little fingers, and flicked the button that controlled the music.

The strains of 'Hey Diddle Diddle' filled the room as the cat fiddled, the cow jumped over the moon, the dog laughed and a small dish and spoon moved across the base.

Rosie's eyes grew wide and she clapped her hands when it had finished. 'Again, Daddy. Play it again.'

Virgil flicked the switch over to the night-time song and soon the strains of Brahms' 'Lullaby' filled the room.

Rosie clapped her hands again. Although the characters continued to move in the same way, the music was softer and more peaceful.

Virgil yawned and stretched and Clara laughed.

'It definitely works for Daddy,' he told Rosie with a grin, then tickled his daughter.

The girl giggled, the sound making Clara fall in love with the child.

'Thanks, Clara.'

She flicked her attention from Rosie to Virgil, who was smiling at her in the way that had often made her knees weaken. Now was no exception.

'It's a wonderful gift.'

'My pleasure.' Their gazes held for a moment. Both seemed to be remembering happier times—times they'd shared together.

When the music began for the third time, Virgil groaned and switched it off.

'More, please. More, Daddy.'

'Later. It's time for dinner now. Say thank you to Clara.'

'Thank you, Clara,' Rosie repeated.

'You're welcome,' Clara replied.

'I presume both tunes are on continuous play?' Virgil asked. When Clara nodded he groaned.

'And I made sure I put long-life batteries in.' Her smile was wide.

'How considerate,' he teased, and winked at her.

The action caused her heart to skip a beat, and she knew that as she was already instantly enthralled with his daughter, she'd do well to keep guarding her heart against becoming enthralled with Rosie's father.

CHAPTER SIX

'SORRY FOR THE slight delay,' Gwenda announced as she came through the swinging door from the kitchen. She carried a large tray with steaming plates. Placing them on the table she said, 'Sit down, before it gets cold. Virgil, can you pour the wine, please?'

Virgil instantly reached for the bottle of white wine that stood chilling in a silver bucket. He wiped the base and offered it to Clara. 'Wine?'

'Yes, please.'

He poured one for himself and one for Gwenda, before passing Rosie a sippy cup of water. Clara watched as the three-year-old fed herself quite well, sometimes using the fork and spoon as well as her fingers. If the food was too hot she would blow on it, or ask her daddy to blow on it for her. The child was incredibly adorable.

The conversation over dinner was kept rolling by Gwenda, who explained that she'd known Virgil all his life and that she'd been more than happy to come and help him out after his wife had passed away.

Rosie also offered several topics of conversation such as not wanting to eat her carrots, demanding sauce on everything, and wanting Clara to help her finish the final three mouthfuls.

'You don't have to. I can do it,' Virgil told her.

'It's fine. I'm more than happy to help. I often help Arthur and Maybelle with their twins.'

'Aunty Clara to the rescue, eh?'

Her answer was a tinkling laugh and Virgil had to stop himself from staring at her. When she laughed, it illuminated her entire face and made her look radiant. He liked making her laugh. He liked being near her, watching her graceful movements, and he was pleased at the way both Rosie and Gwenda seemed to like this very special woman.

Rosie dropped her spoon on the floor and he quickly bent to retrieve it. 'There you are, funny face.'

Rosie giggled and blew a kiss to her beloved daddy.

As he continued to watch the way Clara interacted with Rosie, he couldn't help but wonder what might have happened if he hadn't taken that position in Montreal. Would they have stayed together as they'd planned? Would both of them have found fulfilment in their careers? Would they now be married with a gaggle of children? Would Clara still have had her accident and had to endure so much pain?

It was stupid to play the 'what if' game because there was no way he could go back and change the past, but he could most definitely change the future.

Once Rosie had finished eating it was time for her bath. Clara thanked Gwenda for the delicious meal, and when Gwenda headed to the kitchen with the first load of dishes Clara instantly stood and began helping to clear.

'You don't have to do that,' Virgil stated. 'You're a guest.'

'Oh, piffle. With our history, I'm hardly a *real* guest,' Clara stated as she took the next load of dishes through to the kitchen.

Virgil conceded she had a point. The fact that they'd known each other for almost two decades meant that she didn't expect to be treated like a true first-time guest. He was glad, in a way, because it meant she felt comfortable—not only around Gwenda and Rosie, but around him.

While Clara and Gwenda cleared he helped Rosie from her booster seat and went to start her bath. He could hear Gwenda and Clara chatting in the kitchen before Gwenda gave Clara directions to Rosie's bedroom. Then he heard his daughter showing Clara around her bedroom, introducing her soft toys.

With the bath running, Virgil walked to Rosie's room, leaning on the doorframe and watching the two of them together.

'This is my tea set. I play with my toys and have tea parties, but Gwenda says that I have to have 'maginary food and drink only—no real food and drink.'

'That's a good idea,' Clara agreed as another teddy bear and a doll were shoved into her hands for inspection. 'Imaginary food and drink means you don't get any ants in your bedroom.'

''Sactly! And Daddy sits down on the blanket and he drinks his tea with his little finger in the air.' Rosie burst into a fit of giggles at this, and held the cup in her hand and tried desperately to hold it with her little finger in the air. 'And he makes slurpy noises.'

Rosie slurped, clearly to ensure Clara understood what she meant. Clara laughed and lifted a small cup to her lips, putting her little finger in the air and making slurping noises, causing Rosie to laugh even more.

It warmed his heart to see them interact like his. She was so natural with Rosie—so open and accepting. His hope began to increase once more that Clara might one day change the nature of their relationship and allow him to court her properly. That was a mistake he'd made the first time. They'd gone from being friends to being a couple without all the lovely in-between moments of really finding the romance within their relationship.

When he'd decided upon this course of action—to see whether he could find a future with Clara—he'd been surprised to discover she hadn't married. Of course, back then, he hadn't known about her accident and months of rehab, but even still, she might have met someone when she'd been overseas.

Now, getting to know this new Clara, he had to admit that she was far more content and confident within her own life than she'd ever been in the past. She'd always had that inner strength, but now she had the confidence to use it. It was great to see and very alluring.

As Rosie started to show Clara her favourite story books Virgil cleared his throat. 'Bathtime, Rosie.'

'Non, non, non!'

Rosie quickly tried to climb onto the bed behind Clara, but Virgil was too fast for her and came into the room, scooping her up in his arms. Then he started to blow raspberries onto her tummy, making Rosie squeal loudly with delight. The child's infectious laughter filled the room with vibrancy and colour, making Virgil and Clara laugh as well.

'Arrêtes, Papa!' she ordered between giggles, not meaning a word she said.

Virgil repeated the action, the sound of his lips on her stomach echoing around the room as Rosie's laughter bubbled over.

'Ready to get drenched?' Virgil asked Clara as he led the procession to the bathroom.

The tub had been half filled with water and was covered with foaming masses of white bubbles. Virgil tested the water and, after ensuring it wouldn't burn Rosie's delicate skin, shut the taps off and went to undress his daughter. Surprisingly, he found Clara helping Rosie to get her T-shirt over her head.

'Thanks.'

Clara grinned at him. 'I'm an experienced aunty, remember?'

'I can see that.' He grinned as he helped the little girl into the bath.

Rosie searched for her toys amongst the bubbles, enjoying a game that was obviously a nightly ritual. She pulled out cups and boats and animals, delighting in each find. The two adults stood side by side, watching the child play.

'She's gorgeous, Virgil. I didn't expect her to be bilingual.'

'That's because most three-year-olds aren't. But I want her to continue to be raised speaking both languages.'

'You talk to her in both French and English?'

'Yes, but since we returned to Australia last year, she's really started to pick up the Aussie twang.'

Clara was surprised. 'You left Montreal last year?'

He nodded and beckoned her out into the hallway. That way they could talk without disturbing Rosie.

'Rosie was only six months old when Diana passed away, and for a while I wasn't sure what to do. Diana had no family in Canada, and as a qualified surgeon, I knew I could get work anywhere. Gwenda came over and lived with us, taking care of Rosie so I could work, but Gwenda doesn't speak much French so it was difficult for her. I took a locum position at Sydney General for six months, so we could acclimatise ourselves to the Australian climate, and after that Victoria seemed like the logical choice. My parents are here, when they're not travelling, so after giving it much thought, I decided to move back to the last place I could remember being really happy.'

He looked into her upturned face and couldn't resist brushing a strand of hair from her face, tucking it behind her ear.

They stood like that for a long moment, staring into each other's eyes, unsure what to say or do next. What he wanted to do was to gather her into his arms, hold her as close as possible and press his lips to hers—but he'd promised her they would remain friends. *Friends.* He knew that if all Clara could ever give him was friendship, then he would take it. Of course he wanted more—he was a red-blooded male in love with this incredible woman—but it was because he loved her and respected her that he knew he would accept whatever verdict she gave on the status of their relationship.

'Sounds as though you've had a few difficult years.' Clara was the first to speak, the first to break eye contact and glance over at Rosie, playing happily in the bath.

'I think we both have,' he added. 'The question is, where do we go from here?'

He couldn't help but look at her lips as he spoke, remembering all too vividly just how incredible it had been to kiss that mouth. In the past, their lips had meshed with perfect synchronicity. Would it be the same now?

When she looked at him again, he was positive he saw repressed desire in her eyes. Was that possible? Did Clara *want* him to kiss her? When she stared at his lips before meeting his gaze once more, he was certain those were the signals she was sending.

'I—I don't know.'

The words were barely a whisper, but he heard them. Virgil cleared his throat, needing to break this moment, needing to take things slowly even though he wanted nothing more than to follow through on that urge. Clara followed suit, both of them turning their attention to the little girl still enjoying playing with her toys in the bath.

'Rosie means the world to me, Clara. I've cut my workload in half so we can have more time together. It was one of the major reasons for moving back to Loggeen. I loved growing up here, and I know it's the best thing for Rosie. She'll make close friends, have people watching out for her, caring about her. It will make a vast difference to her life,' Virgil continued.

Rosie looked across at both of them, standing outside the bathroom, and held out her hands to them. 'Look! Look!'

Both adults went into the bathroom and over to the tub. Clara crouched down and looked at the toy Rosie was holding out to her.

'Oooh! A turtle. What's his name?'

'Mr Turtle,' Rosie said, as though that was completely obvious.

While Clara was inspecting Mr Turtle, Rosie took great delight in bringing one hand firmly down onto the surface of the water.

Splash!

With one single motion they were thoroughly wet. They both laughed, which made Rosie think she should do it again.

'Funny!' She giggled before splashing once more.

'I think that's enough, scallywag.' Virgil smiled but spoke firmly, so the child understood he wasn't playing games.

'She'd get along so well with my nieces. Mischief. All three of them are pure mischief.'

'It would be great to meet them,' Virgil said as he reached into the bath for a washcloth and began quickly washing his daughter. 'Gwenda's enrolled Rosie in a play-group, but that's only one day a week. Meeting other children would be really good.'

'I'll call Maybelle and get her to set up a play date.'

'Sounds fun—I think?'

'What? Three little girls aged three and under? Sounds like madness to me!'

She laughed, and the sound washed over him like the breeze on a fresh summer's day. He marvelled at how nat-

ural Clara was with his daughter. He watched the way she
scooped his daughter carefully out of the bath and wrapped
her in the waiting towel before drawing Rosie closer.

'Cuddle this little girl dry!'

She wriggled Rosie from side to side, making the child
laugh. The sound was music to his heart.

'Come on—let's get you to your room and dressed for
bed.'

Gwenda was ready and waiting to take over. Rosie's
arms went out to her and she smiled gleefully. Clara
watched as Gwenda quickly dried and dressed the wrig-
gling toddler, amazed at the other woman's speed at performing the task.

'Give Daddy a kiss goodnight,' Gwenda instructed, and
Rosie instantly puckered her little lips for her father. 'And a
cuddle and kiss for Clara.' That was Gwenda's next order.

Rosie eyed Clara briefly, before holding out her arms
for a cuddle. A lump caught in Clara's throat as she held
the child tenderly, closing her eyes to savour the moment.

A kiss was placed on her cheek, then Rosie marched
back into the bathroom proclaiming, 'Teef time,' and
waited patiently for Gwenda to hand her the toothbrush.

'Goodnight, darling.' Virgil kissed her again and mo-
tioned for Clara to leave.

'Don't you put her to bed?' Clara asked as they walked
downstairs.

'Usually—but tonight, considering you're here, Gwenda
will do it.'

'Please,' Clara implored, 'I don't want to disrupt the
routine. You go back up and I'll let myself out.'

'Just like that—you're leaving?' He quirked an eyebrow at her.

Clara shrugged and looked down at her hands. 'I think
I should.'

There had already been several moments tonight when

she'd fallen in thrall to Virgil Arterton once again. Hadn't she given herself a stern lecture before she'd arrived? Hadn't she told herself to keep her distance and not let his natural boyish charm infect her? Yet when they'd been standing in the hallway outside the bathroom, all she'd wanted was to feel the touch of his lips on hers, to taste the delight only he had been able to give her, to breathe in his scent and allow herself to drown in it.

Virgil really was as dangerous to her sense of self-preservation as she'd expected. The fact that after all this time, she'd only tonight realised she still wasn't over him, was perhaps the revelation she'd needed in order to find the strength to leave his presence.

'But why? Why do you need to rush off?' He reached out and took her hand gently in his own.

Clara bit her lip. If she told him the truth he would know she wasn't over him. He would know that the instant she'd seen him again, her heart had leapt with joy and delight but she'd quashed it. It was true things hadn't turned out the way either of them had wanted, but the past was the past and the present was the present—and hopefully the present might lead to a future she'd often dreamed about.

Was it possible? Was it really possible that she and Virgil could have a fresh start?

Everything he'd done and said since returning to Loggeen—the way he treated the staff he worked with, the way he was thoughtful and considerate of his patients, not to mention his doting daddy routine with Rosie—all of it, every aspect of his personality, was showing her that he *had* changed.

Even the way he was now holding her hand, stroking her skin while gazing into her eyes as though he really couldn't get enough of her, rather than just taking charge of the situation, was different. He was letting her choose whether this was the road she wanted to take. He was proving that he'd listened to her when she'd said she just wanted to be friends.

She *did* want to be friends, but was it wrong for her to want more? If they changed the nature of their friendship wouldn't history simply repeat itself?

Clara swallowed, looking at those blue eyes she'd always loved to stare into. Her mind was in turmoil, her body betraying every rational thought she had, in its need for the man before her.

'Virgil...' His name was a whispered caress and her heart began to pound even more wildly against her chest as he closed the distance between them.

They were standing at the bottom of the stairs, the lounge room in one direction, the front door in the other. She should leave. She knew she should leave. But that was her head talking, not her heart. Her heart was hammering out a rhythm which wanted to urge him closer, urge him to lower his head, urge him to kiss her just as he had so many times in the past.

'Clara?'

Her name was a question upon his lips, and she knew Virgil was offering her a way out of this bubble filled with desire and need, which seemed to have captured both of them.

She couldn't move. She didn't want to. She wanted this. She wanted to kiss him. And, if she was honest with herself, she was curious to see whether the magic which had flared between them so many years ago, was still present.

'Clara...' He murmured her name again. 'If you keep standing here I'm not going to be able to resist you.'

His words only fuelled the fire within her.

'There are too many...' She paused, her words breathless, her tone filled with repressed desire as she gazed longingly at his mouth once more.

He was *her* Virgil. He'd burst back into her life and

turned her contented world upside down. How was she supposed to resist him when he looked so perfect? When he smelled so good? When he was being the perfect gentleman and allowing her to choose what happened next? What would happen if she did kiss him now? What would it change?

The answer came hard and fast after the question. It would change *everything*—and Clara wasn't sure she was ready for that.

'Virgil…' She breathed his name again, then closed her eyes and found the superhuman strength from somewhere to edge backwards. Swallowing, she looked into his handsome face, shaking her head. 'I need—' She licked her dry lips. 'I need more time.'

His gaze dropped to encompass her lips one last time before he nodded and brought her hand to his lips, pressing a long, tender kiss to her knuckles.

'Take all the time you need. I'm not going anywhere.'

CHAPTER SEVEN

'WHY AREN'T YOU in your bed? You're supposed to be sleeping by now.' Clara spoke lovingly to her dog as she entered her apartment.

Darling Juzzy always insisted on greeting her whenever she came home, and tonight Clara really needed it.

'I'm so confused, Juzzy,' she told the dog as she checked Juzzy's automatic food, and bubbling water dispensers. Yes, Juzzy had enough food and fresh water. As Clara continued to talk, the dog followed her around the apartment. 'One minute I think everything is going great between myself and Virgil, and the next I just don't know.'

As Clara prepared for bed she thought back to those intense moments she'd shared with Virgil at the bottom of the staircase. How was it possible that the man could still get her all hot and bothered with only one look?

It was a look that said, *I want you, Clara. I need you, Clara. I adore you, Clara.* How could one glance say so much and cause her to forget her resolve to remain as friends? She couldn't believe how tempted she'd been to close the distance between them and press her lips to his. He had been waiting for her to do just that, but when she'd moved back, deciding not to follow through on the impulse, he hadn't made any effort to talk her round as he would have in the past. He'd let her take control of the situation and it had only made her appreciate him more.

Getting involved in a romantic relationship with him would make her life way more complicated than it needed to be. Wasn't she in a good place with her life? Wasn't she happy? She'd told Virgil only a few weeks ago that she was more than content with her life, but now here she was questioning that decision. Yes, she was pleased with how she'd managed to pull her life back together, but what if there was *more* happiness just waiting for her to claim it? What if being with Virgil was her destiny?

Then there was Rosie. Virgil's gorgeous daughter had stolen her heart, so what would happen if things progressed between them and Rosie became attached? That would be all well and good if everything worked out between herself and Virgil, but given their history there was no guarantee.

The last thing Clara wanted to do was to hurt the child, but the real question was, could she completely trust Virgil again? Would he turn on her as he had in the past? If she made a decision he didn't agree with, would he try persuading her to change her mind? She'd stood her ground last time, and she'd do it again, but would she be able to cope with yet another heartbreak? She wasn't so sure.

'Am I overreacting?' she asked the dog as she finished brushing her teeth and climbed beneath the covers.

Juzzy looked up at her expectantly, and when Clara gave in and patted the bedcovers beside her, the dog climbed up the little step stool and jumped up onto the bed, snuggling next to Clara.

She stroked the dog, the rhythmic movements helping her to relax. 'I like him, Juzzy. I like this new and improved version of Virgil. And if this is our second chance—well, I don't want to blow it.'

There was still a long way to go—a lot of things which

needed to be discussed. She needed to tell him about the outcome of her devastating accident and just how it had changed the course of her life. Yes, it had taken a lot of re-habilitation to put herself back together, but with the help of her family and close friends she'd managed it. Yes, there were lasting devastating repercussions, and, yes, those is-sues might be detrimental to the rekindling of the fright-eningly natural chemistry which seemed to exist between herself and Virgil.

If things were going to get permanently serious between them, she needed to know how he felt about having more children. She wanted children. She really did, but due to the accident her badly crushed pelvis and subsequent sur-geries had put paid to any possibility of her ever carrying a child. Clara had endured several years of both physical and psychological therapy in order to recover from the effects of the accident—the main one being that to start with, she'd felt less of a woman simply because she'd never have children.

'You don't need to carry a child inside you and give birth just to prove you're a woman,' her psychologist had told her. 'Many women don't go through the trauma you've endured—women who, medically, have nothing wrong with them—and yet they still can't conceive naturally. You're not alone in the way you feel, Clara. In fact, given the extent of your injuries, it's a miracle you're walking. Perhaps you need to cut yourself some slack…be a bit kinder to yourself. Not all women need children to com-plete their lives.'

The problem was she *did*, and spending time with her nieces and Rosie only intensified that sensation. Being with Virgil's little girl, hearing her giggle, seeing the way she wrapped her arms around her father's neck and pressed wet and sloppy kisses to his cheek, had only made her yearn to have a little mischief-maker of her own—hers and Virgil's.

That had always been the plan. The two of them together. The two of them getting married and raising a family. That had been all she'd wanted for so long, and now—now that there was the slightest possibility it might happen—she was scared that should Virgil learn the truth, learn that she could never have children, he might reject her for a second time.

'You're borrowing trouble,' she told herself aloud as she switched on the radio, allowing the soothing classical music being played to calm her mind.

She needed to sleep, and in order to do that she needed to shut her mind down—and that meant she needed to stop worrying about what might or might not happen with Virgil.

'Easier said than done,' she whispered to Juzzy.

For the next week Clara made sure she was polite and professional every time she came into contact with Virgil. It wasn't that she was trying to avoid him, but rather she was trying to come to terms with the numerous events which had happened since he'd re-entered her life. She'd tried not to overthink the time they'd already spent together, which was difficult for her as her family had used to joke that she should hold a degree in overthinking things.

If things were going to move smoothly between herself and the gorgeous man working alongside her, then Clara knew she needed to relax more.

It wasn't until she was doing her second Saturday night shift at the hospital that he caught up with her. It was just after eleven p.m., and he'd been in Theatre for the past five hours with a motor vehicle accident patient. He was still in scrubs as he walked over to the nurses' station, where she was busy typing information into the computer, and slumped down into the chair beside her.

'So, have you been avoiding me or have we both just been insanely busy this past week?'

'Definitely busy—although I *have* enjoyed our game of voicemail tag.'

He chuckled at her words, then looked around the ED. 'Slow night?'

'Shh.' She frowned. 'Don't ever say that. Saying that is like begging for a horde of patients to come bursting through the doors.'

'Well, they wouldn't exactly *burst*,' he pointed out. 'They'd have to go through triage first, and then sit in the waiting room for—'

'Stop being so pedantic,' she interrupted. 'How's Rosie?'

Changing the subject to his daughter was a good distraction. Clara was able to finish entering the information into the computer before saving the files. Once that was done she began clearing up the desk in front of her, needing to do something to distract her from Virgil's close proximity. How could the man still smell so sexy after such a long stint in Theatre?

'She's settling in well. Your sister-in-law got in touch with Gwenda, and I think they've arranged a play date for tomorrow. Thanks for mentioning it to Maybelle. The more little friends Rosie can make, the better—and, besides, I'm looking forward to meeting them.'

He passed Clara a few paperclips which were on the long desk, close to where he was sitting. She accepted them with a nod and put them into the paperclip container, ensuring their hands didn't touch so she wouldn't have to endure that overpowering zing of awareness which occurred every time Virgil's fingers came into contact with hers.

'Is Rosie excited to meet the twins?'

'She is—and it'll do her good to learn to share her toys.'

'Is she enjoying the clock?'

'Oh, she loves it. You chose a winner there. Although both those songs have become permanently lodged in my psyche and I've found myself humming Brahms' "Lullaby" several times of a morning.' He tapped the side of head with the heel of his hand, as though trying to dislodge the ear worm.

'Glad to be of service!' She laughed.

The desk was now shipshape and everything was tidied away. What could she do next to distract her? His nearness was already creating havoc with her senses, and it was all she could do not to stop herself from leaning close to him and doing the one thing she'd been dreaming about for the past week—pressing a kiss to his lips. Didn't the man realise just how addictive he could be?

'Do you give your nieces piles of noisy toys?'

'Of course. It's an aunty's responsibility.'

Virgil chuckled again. 'I'm sure Arthur is looking forward to getting his own back when you start having children.'

The smile instantly slid from Clara's face and she quickly stood. 'I should go and check on the patients in the treatment bays. That way, when a horde of emergencies come flooding in—thanks to your earlier comment—' she tried to keep a light and teasing tone to her voice, but even to her own ears she knew she hadn't succeeded '—the rounds will have been done.'

'Hey.' Virgil stood and put a hand gently on her arm. She tried not to gasp as the zing of desire spread up her arm and burst throughout her body. 'Clara, what's wrong?'

'Nothing. Just doing my job.' She forced a smile and took a step away.

Virgil instantly dropped his hand and let her go. What had he said? Did Clara not want children of her own? If that was the case, how did he feel about that? With the re-emergence of Clara into his life, his hopes of having more children had increased. It wasn't just that he wanted to spend the rest of his life with Clara, he wanted to build a family with her. Was that wanting too much?

After the successful dinner at his house last weekend, when that moment at the bottom of the stairs had shown him that she was as captivated with him as he was with her, his hopes had continued to increase. Still, he needed to be aware of Clara's own feelings, to *listen* to her and take his cues from her.

He'd been wanting all week to ask her for another date—one on which Rosie would be able to join them so she could get to know his daughter better. Rosie was such an integral part of his life that he wanted his little love to be as comfortable around Clara as he was—but would Clara be happy to go on a date with himself and a three-year-old? She and Rosie had connected beautifully last weekend, but had that been just a one-off? If Clara saw Rosie having a temper tantrum, would that put her off wanting to get involved with him? Especially if she *didn't* want to have children in the future?

The phone on the desk rang, and as he was the closest he picked it up. 'Emergency Department,' he said, then reached for a pen in order to note the details from the paramedics.

An elderly woman had injured both ankles after a fall from a stepladder. Both she and her elderly husband, who was in a wheelchair, were being brought in via ambulance. Estimated time of arrival was ten minutes. After hanging up the phone, he went in search of Clara, finding her just finishing off checking on the three patients who were presently being monitored for a variety of injuries.

'Ambulance arriving in just under ten minutes,' he said, and gave her the details. 'Do you need help?'

She shook her head. 'Should be fine. Besides, we have enough staff here to deal with a non-life-threatening emergency—which this is.' She headed back to the nurses' station. 'I'll call the orthopaedic registrar for a consult on her ankles, but until we've been through the X-ray process there's no urgency.'

'See? My earlier gaffe didn't result in a horde of emergencies,' he pointed out, and was rewarded with quizzical smile.

'Not yet.'

Virgil knew he should go home, but he'd just finished a five-hour emergency surgery, missing the opportunity to say goodnight on the phone to Rosie, so there was no reason for him to dash home. If he was honest with himself, what he really wanted to do was stay here with Clara.

When the ambulance arrived he stayed out of the way, watching as the patient's husband, still in his wheelchair, was lowered to the ground via the hydraulic lift before an orderly pushed him inside. The paramedics soon followed, with the stretcher holding the man's wife.

'Henry hates to leave me and I hate to leave him,' Clara's patient, Mrs Linda Santorino, told her as the paramedics took her into a treatment room. 'We've been through so much during our lives, and now, as we're coming to the end of our race, we really do like doing things together.'

'That's lovely to hear,' Clara responded as she got into position, ready to transfer Mrs Santorino from the paramedic stretcher to the hospital barouche.

When Virgil came to stand next to her, ready to help, she found it momentarily difficult to concentrate on what she needed to do. Why wouldn't he go home? He wasn't supposed to be here, driving her to distraction.

'One, two, *three*,' the paramedic counted.

They shifted Mrs Santorino—or Linda, as she'd invited them all to call her—onto the hospital bed. The paramedics finished giving their handover, letting Clara know what pain relief had already been administered, and Clara started her own assessment of the patient. After a brief clinical assessment of Linda's ankles, Clara requested X-rays and a few pathology tests.

'Both ankles are most definitely sprained, but as they're so swollen I'm unable to assess whether they're broken. The X-rays will tell us more.'

'Once she's had the X-rays, can we go home?' Henry asked, coughing a little as he spoke.

Clara eyed him carefully. His skin was pale and his lips seemed a little dry.

'I'm afraid Linda will need to stay in for at least a day or two.'

'What?' Linda seemed surprised at this. 'But—but even if I have to stay off my feet, I can still go home, can't I? We're set up with wheelchair ramps and everything for Henry, so surely I can just hire myself a wheelchair and head back home?'

There was a hint of desperation in Linda's tone and Clara really felt for them. It must be so difficult to get to a stage in your life, when your mind was as sharp as ever but your body was starting to fail you.

'Henry can't be at home on his own. I'm his full-time carer.'

'Oh. Uh—do you have any family close by who could perhaps come and help out?' Virgil asked, but both of them shook their head.

'Well, why don't we see what the X-rays reveal and we can plan from there?' Clara stated, not wanting to upset either of them. 'In the meantime—Henry, can I get you a cup of tea?'

The elderly man's eyes softened at her words. 'That would be great, love. Thanks.'

'I can do that,' Virgil offered. 'I'll even see if I can find a few biscuits for you, Henry.'

'Thanks, lad.' Henry nodded.

'Do *I* get a cuppa?' Linda asked hopefully.

'I'd rather you don't have anything at this present time,' Clara told her patient. 'At least until I get the results of your scans.'

She didn't want to tell them that if Linda's ankles were broken, there was a high possibility that surgery would be required.

'What are you *doing*?' Clara asked Virgil in a stage whisper as they headed back to the nurses' station. 'You're not the tea lady.'

'And neither are you. The brilliant volunteers who do our tea runs are well and truly off duty and the nurses have other things to do right now. Besides, I don't mind.'

Clara sighed heavily. 'Just go home, Virgil.'

'Why? Rosie's asleep. Gwenda's probably asleep. I have a lot of energy at the moment. I don't mind helping out.'

She rolled her eyes. 'Ugh! I give up. Right. Go make the tea for Henry. I need to get these X-rays and tests sorted out.'

She turned her back on him, deciding that he could do whatever he wanted. She wasn't in charge of the ED, her brother was, and at present Arthur wasn't there—so far be it from her to dictate what Victory Hospital's leading general surgeon should and shouldn't do!

The orderlies came and wheeled Linda's barouche to the radiology department. Clara had thought Henry would want to go with her, but when she went to check on him he was sitting in his wheelchair, sipping his cup of tea. Virgil was seated nearby, chatting amicably.

'Comfy?' she asked.

'Absolutely. Henry was just telling me that he used to be in the Air Force.'

'Over thirty years,' Henry added. 'Plane went down twice and I survived both times.' He took a bite of biscuit and when he started to chew, he coughed at the same time, breathing in and getting some biscuit lodged in his throat.

'Henry?' Clara watched him closely.

The man coughed again.

'You OK?'

She came closer and Virgil stood up from his chair, both of them on alert to see if Henry needed help. He tried to suck in some air but it was clearly difficult for him. The elderly man's eyes widened in terror as he tried to breathe once more. He gasped several times, each one a valiant attempt, but it was no good.

Although time seemed to have stood still, it was only a matter of seconds before Clara and Virgil were by Henry's side. Clara hit Henry firmly on the back, hoping to dislodge the obstruction. It didn't work.

'Help me get him out of the wheelchair.' Clara ensured the wheels were locked in place as Virgil put both his arms beneath Henry's armpits and performed the Heimlich manoeuvre.

Nothing!

Clara pressed the emergency button, alerting staff that they required help.

'There's no way to dislodge it,' she told Virgil. 'Get me a barouche,' she told the first nurse who appeared in the treatment room. 'His glands are starting to swell,' she announced.

'I'll need to do a tracheotomy,' Virgil stated as Henry tried desperately to breathe.

Only the smallest amount of air was getting through. The elderly man looked even more frail than before, and Clara was exceedingly worried for him.

'Set up for emergency tracheotomy,' she told Kate, the sister in charge this evening. 'Let's get Henry onto the bed,' she added when a barouche was wheeled in from another room.

Staff were helping out everywhere. A tray was set up for Virgil to use while he pulled on a pair of gloves. Clara placed her hands on either side of Henry's head to keep him as still as possible, seeing the look in the man's eyes conveying his distress at finding himself in such a situation.

'It's OK, Henry. You'll be fine in no time. Virgil's one of our finest surgeons and he's going to take excellent care of you.'

'Yes, I am,' he stated firmly as he carefully palpated the tracheal rings, ensuring he made the incision into the correct space. 'Scalpel,' he stated, and Kate put the instrument into his hand.

A moment later Virgil had a piece of tubing in place and with a gurgling, rasping sound Henry was able successfully to get air into his lungs. Clara breathed a sigh of relief, very happy now that Virgil had indeed stuck around. It wasn't that she wouldn't have been able to perform the emergency procedure, but it was much better to have a surgeon do it.

Now that Henry was breathing, Virgil turned and thanked the staff. 'I think we'll transfer Henry to one of the emergency bays,' he said. 'So that when Linda comes back there's room for her here. Besides, the emergency bays have the equipment needed to completely remove this obstruction. Kate, can you get me the anaesthetics registrar, please? Given Henry's age, we'll need to sedate him in order to successfully remove the obstruction.'

'Let's get you something for the pain,' Clara said.

Thankfully, Henry was wearing a medical alert bracelet on his wrist, and after checking the information contained there, she was able to draw up some analgesics for Henry to assist him with his immediate pain.

When Henry was in the emergency bay, which was

bigger and had more equipment, the anaesthetics registrar came and consulted alongside Virgil. It was decided, due to Henry's age, not to give him a full sedative. A local would be enough to keep Henry relaxed enough for Virgil to use the equipment to dislodge the obstruction.

Once they began, the procedure didn't take long, and when Linda came back from the radiology department Clara explained the situation to her.

'So where is Henry now?' a shocked Linda asked.

'He's being admitted to a ward for observation,' Clara told her as she checked the scans of Linda's ankles. 'I'm very happy to tell you that neither of your ankles are broken, just very badly sprained. You're going to need a lot of bed-rest as well as physiotherapy for the next few months.'

'Months?' Linda laid her head back against the pillows and promptly burst into tears. It was all too much for her.

'We'll be admitting you tonight, and I'll do my best to ensure you and Henry are side by side in the ward.' Clara gave Linda a tissue and wrote up a prescription for more pain relief. 'I'll be around to see you in the morning.'

'And you'll look after my treatment?'

Clara shook her head. 'You're being admitted under one of our physicians—Dr Presley. He'll also be around in the morning to introduce himself to you. You'll love him. He was an Air Force doctor for many years.'

'Oh, well. If he was Air Force...' Linda let her words trail off as she wiped her eyes and blew her nose. 'It's going to be a bit of an upheaval, but Henry and I can get through it.'

Now that she'd had her cry, it was as though Linda was ready to cope with the latest challenge in her life.

'What an amazing woman,' Clara said to Virgil when they both ended up back at the nurses' station.

'What an amazing *couple*,' Virgil agreed. 'So devoted to each other.'

'Linda must have been through a lot of hard times during her life—especially as Henry said he'd gone down with his plane twice!'

'It would have been difficult for her.' Virgil sat back in his chair, resting his head and closing his eyes. 'He'd head off to work on a top secret Air Force mission and she'd probably have no idea whether he was dead or alive until he walked in the front door.'

'I don't know if I could live like that—not knowing what was happening to the people I loved.'

'That's how I used to feel whenever I thought about you.'

Virgil's words were soft and Clara couldn't help but stare at him.

'What?'

'I used to think about you a lot, Clara.'

'Even when you were married?'

He smiled sadly. 'Thinking about an old girlfriend isn't a crime—even for a married man.'

'What happened?' she asked softly, pleased that the ED was indeed quiet and there weren't a lot of staff around. 'You said your wife died in a car accident with her lover. That must have brought you a lot of mixed emotions.'

'It did. When a person gets married, no one ever thinks their happiness is going to change—but it can and it does. I think Diana was fed up with me spending so much time at the hospital, devoting more time to my patients than to her. She was right, though. I *did* spend too much time at the hospital because I wasn't happy in my marriage.'

'Why weren't you happy?'

He met and held her gaze. 'Because I married the wrong woman.' He shook his head sadly. 'I tried to make it work. You'd rejected me—or so I thought—and I needed to get on with my life. Diana and I went to marriage counselling and things actually turned around for a while. It was good. It was happy. And she became pregnant with Rosie.'

Virgil exhaled slowly and shook his head.

'But Diana had a bad pregnancy. She was sick. Gestational diabetes, pre-eclampsia—the works. She was bedridden from five months onwards, and when Rosie was born via emergency C-section...' He shook his head again. 'Diana didn't bond with her. She didn't want to hold her, feed her, look at her.'

'Oh, Virgil. How sad...'

'When they returned home from the hospital, Diana still couldn't attach herself to Rosie. I took several months off work so I could care for the baby—feeding, changing, bathing...I was Daddy, and caring for Rosie was the most important job I'd ever had. Diana...' He trailed off. 'I didn't know she was seeing someone else. He was one of the district nurses who had been coming around to check on her during her third trimester. Both of them were killed outright when the car hit a tree.'

Clara gasped and covered her mouth with her hand.

'She was leaving me. That's where the two of them had been going. Off to start a new life together.' He held his palms up and shrugged. 'She'd left me a note saying it was over. She didn't want custody of Rosie, and she didn't want to be married to me. She wanted to be happy, and I wasn't the man to make her happy.'

'Oh, Virgil.' Clara shook her head and within the next instant she'd thrown her arms around him, hugging him close. 'I wish I'd been there to help you through those times.'

He eased back a little and looked into her face. 'I wish I'd been there to help you through *your* bad times.'

When Clara continued to stare into his eyes, wanting to convey her desire to support him, there was only one way she could think of to do that—she pressed her mouth to his.

CHAPTER EIGHT

VIRGIL COULDN'T BELIEVE the way it felt to have her lips pressed to his once again, but no sooner had she kissed him than he put his hands on her shoulders and eased her away. 'Not here,' he whispered. 'I don't want to give the gossipers any ammunition.'

Clara's eyes went from being glazed over with a mixture of sadness, regret and desire to widening in shock, as she realised exactly what she'd done and where they were presently situated.

'Oh, my gosh!' She sprang back from him and stood. 'I'm— I'm—' She shook her head.

Virgil stood, but kept his distance. 'It's OK.' He glanced around them. 'No one saw.'

He could feel fatigue starting to set in, and unsuccessfully smothered a yawn.

'Perhaps you should head home and get some rest. If Rosie's anything like my nieces, she wakes up early.'

'That she does—and she loves coming into Daddy's bed to cuddle him for a few minutes and then jump on him for half an hour in an effort to ensure he's really awake.'

Clara laughed. He liked seeing her smile.

'Listen, are you free tomorrow afternoon? I know you'll be here until the morning shift arrives, and then you'll need to sleep, but after that—'

Clara shook her head. 'I'm looking after the girls to-morrow afternoon and evening. Maybelle has a shift, and Arthur's away this weekend in Sydney at a conference.'

'How about next weekend?'

She hesitated. 'What did you have in mind?'

'Perhaps a picnic in the park. You, me and Rosie.'

'Can I bring my dog? Fuzzy-Juzzy loves the park.'

Virgil grinned, realising she couldn't have given him a better response to his invitation. 'I'd love to meet your dog—as, I'm sure, would Rosie.'

'OK, well—emergencies permitting—it's a date.'

Virgil reached for her hand, giving it a little squeeze. 'It's a date,' he reiterated, more than delighted that she was accepting this new level of their relationship.

As he headed home he felt a weight lift from his shoulders. He'd told Clara about his marriage, not hiding from her his own faults in the scenario, and she'd accepted him. He could still feel the burning heat on his lips where hers had brushed his—oh, so gently and filled with compassion.

Yes, they'd both been through a lot, and he knew that whilst Clara had told him she'd been in an accident, she hadn't talked about it further. The fact that she'd been in hospital and rehabilitation for so long could only mean the accident had been quite horrific. The patient he'd operated on earlier tonight would require future surgery, and it made him wonder exactly what Clara's injuries had been.

She might be willing to spend time with him, to get to know his daughter, introduce him to her dog, but that didn't mean she was willing to trust him. He had so much at stake here, and he wanted to do whatever he could to ensure they had the opportunity of a future. But with one wrong move Clara might reject him for ever.

Sure, he'd go on with his life—working, parenting, existing—but without Clara by his side, sharing, laughing, loving, his world would feel like an empty shell. He'd lived that sort of life with Diana, appearing happy on the outside but feeling hollow and broken on the inside. Clara was the only one who could fix him, make him whole again.

He had to continue to hope. Hope that everything would turn out all right in the end and that he and Clara would get their happily-ever-after. Because if they didn't, he knew he'd end up in the pit of despair—and he really didn't want to go back there again.

To say Fuzzy-Juzzy was excited to be going out with her mistress was an understatement.

'I need to take you out more,' she told the dog.

Yes, they went for their daily walks, and if Clara wasn't able to take Juzzy then Maybelle and Arthur would take the Pomeranian whenever they took their own dogs for a walk. Still, having time to take Juzzy to the park was a luxury they were both going to enjoy.

When she arrived at the park, late Saturday afternoon, her clinic and house-calls completed for another week, she saw Virgil pushing Rosie on the swings and couldn't help the instant smile which beamed on her face. She parked her car and came around to the passenger side to get the excited Fuzzy-Juzzy from the back seat. She clipped the leash to Juzzy's collar and headed towards Rosie and Virgil.

'Higher, Daddy!' Rosie was calling.

'Well, well, well. Don't you look lovely?' Virgil stated as Clara walked up to him, reining Juzzy in a little closer to her side. 'Hey, Rosie, look who's here!' Virgil reached out and carefully grabbed the swing, gently slowing it down. 'It's Clara, and she's brought someone new for you to meet.'

When Rosie saw the dog she clapped her hands with delight, and found it difficult to sit still long enough for Virgil to unclip the restraints which had held the little girl firmly in the swing.

'There you go, wriggle-pot,' he said, and helped her to the ground.

Rosie instantly raced over to Clara and Juzzy, running both her small chubby hands through the dog's fur. Juzzy yapped excitedly at this new undivided attention from a little girl. Then the dog was tugging on her leash, as though eager to go for a walk.

'Why don't we take Juzzy for a walk? We have quite a few hours before the sun starts to set.'

'True—and Gwenda made Rosie have a sleep earlier, so my daughter is well rested and can stay up past her bedtime.'

'Yay!' Rosie had clearly overheard the last bit.

'Just for tonight, sweetheart,' he warned as they started walking along the waterfront.

Rosie wanted to have a go at holding Juzzy's leash, and after giving her a lesson in how to hold it, so it didn't hurt her hand, Rosie and Juzzy ran off. Juzzy stopped every now and then to sniff out all sorts of nooks and crannies. It was funny to watch as the dog took the toddler for a walk!

Virgil held out his hand to her. 'May I hold your hand whilst we stroll, ma'am?' he asked, and Clara couldn't help but giggle at his proper, gentlemanly behaviour.

She nodded eagerly and a moment later his soft fingers were laced with her own, the warmth from his touch spreading up her arm to burst throughout her body with delight. They strolled along hand in hand for a while, with Rosie very content to be in charge of the dog but often having a disagreement with Juzzy as to which way they should head next.

Clara knew that if Juzzy started leading Rosie off towards a dangerous path—perhaps towards the lake they were walking around—then all Clara needed to do was give a little whistle and the dog would turn and come

straight to her. Years of puppy school were finally paying off.

When it looked as though Rosie was starting to get tired
they decided to head back towards the car, where Virgil
had left the picnic basket and a rug.

'It is so nice to get away from the hospital and the
clinic,' Clara remarked as they started tucking into the
picnic Gwenda had packed.

Clara had brought some food for Juzzy and the dog was
more than happy to sit near them and eat up.

'And this cold chicken and salad is yummy.'

'Yummy,' Rosie repeated, before Virgil once again told
his daughter not to give the dog her lettuce.

Virgil picked up the bottle of wine and gestured to
Clara's glass. 'More?'

'Just half a glass, please.' Clara lazed back on the rug
and joined him in watching the child eat as though she'd
never been fed before. 'Rosie certainly likes her food. It's
not always easy to get children to eat.'

'She has her days. A few months ago she would only
eat breakfast, so Gwenda made sure it was a breakfast
packed with as many of the five food groups as she could.
Besides, as long as they drink enough fluids, they won't
waste away.'

Clara sighed. 'She really is adorable, Virgil. You are
a lucky man.'

'She's not always such an angel.' He chuckled. 'Sometimes there are smiles all round—the next it's tantrum
after tantrum.'

'Rosie?' Clara joked. 'Have a tantrum?'

Virgil grinned. 'Generally she's a happy little princess,
and one thing I know for sure: she's my little girl and I
wouldn't be without her. I know I finally have my priori-
ties right.'

They sat in a companionable silence as the pressures

of life seemed to ebb away. 'It's so peaceful here,' Clara murmured as Juzzy snuggled up next to her.

A moment later, Rosie decided she wanted to be a dog, like Juzzy, and settled herself down on Clara's lap. Rosie pretended to bark and stick her tongue out, breathing fast like she'd seen Juzzy do.

'Good doggie,' Clara praised, and patted Rosie on the head.

Snuggling in closer, Rosie leaned against Clara, yawning and sighing, clearly displaying her contentment. Clara absorbed the gorgeousness of the child, knowing she would love nothing more than to become a mother to the precious little moppet. The child *and* her daddy were proving far too hard to resist.

'I think she likes you,' Virgil remarked softly as he sipped his wine.

'You think so? Or is she just tired and I was the closest lap for a nap?'

He chuckled. 'Children are honest.'

'And usually have no filter whatsoever,' she added, smiling at him.

It was nice to sit here so content, so relaxed with Virgil and his daughter. If she'd told herself two months ago that she'd be sitting in the park enjoying an evening picnic with Virgil Arterton she never would have believed it. Two months ago she'd been busy going over various scenarios to ensure she and her team were ready for the up and coming retrieval examinations. So much had changed since Virgil had re-entered her life, and she had to admit that she liked spending time with him.

'You look quite content there, with Rosie snuggled against you.'

Clara glanced across at him, his long legs sprawled out in front of him as he propped himself up on his elbow. He was relaxed, charming and sexy.

'Is she falling asleep?'

'Her eyes are closed. She'll become a bit of a dead weight soon.'

'Oh. Do you *want* her to go to sleep?'

He shrugged. 'It'll make putting her in the car a whole lot easier.' He shook his head. 'The other day she went as stiff as a board. It was like she didn't bend any more. Took me almost five minutes to get her arms into the straps and buckle her in safely.'

Clara chuckled. 'They're so funny, these toddlers.' She ran her fingers gently through Rosie's hair.

'Do you want to have any?'

'Toddlers?' she queried, unsure that was what he'd meant.

'Yeah. Babies of your own.'

At his words she looked away, dipping her head down to drop a kiss to the top of Rosie's head, allowing her hair to slide forward and shield her face from his view.

'I mean, I know we talked about getting married and having a family all those years ago, but is that what you still want?'

Clara's mind was starting to slip into panic mode, telling her that she should get out of there as soon as possible, because Virgil was entering dangerous territory. *Just tell him. Just tell him,* her logical side was pushing. *Tell him about your injuries. Tell him about your heartbreak. Tell him—*

'Clara?' There was a hint of confusion in his tone. 'Do you *not* want to have children any more?'

She lifted her head, opened her eyes and tucked her hair behind her ear, knowing she needed to address this with him—but she couldn't do it now.

When they'd first gone out to dinner he'd declared his intentions, which were to woo her back, to spend the rest of his life with her. At the time she'd dismissed it, because she'd thought she'd be able to resist him. She'd been wrong. She'd forgotten how charming he could be. And that was the problem. He'd made her *want* again. He'd made her want to spend the rest of her life with him—with him and Rosie.

And no other children. Because she couldn't give that to him. Yes, they could adopt, but would he want to? Would he be able to love a child that wasn't biologically his? She didn't know, and right now, after the most perfect afternoon, when they'd been happy and relaxed with each other, when they'd laughed and held hands and connected in a way they never had before, she didn't want to ruin it.

'Ugh—you were right about the dead weight part.' She tried to shift. 'I think my legs are lacking blood.'

Clara chuckled, trying to cover up her nervousness. Virgil obliged by kneeling up and lifting Rosie off Clara and into his arms, so the child rested her head on her father's shoulder. Juzzy was also disturbed, and as Clara quickly stood, patting both her legs which were now developing pins and needles, she made sure she had hold of Juzzy's leash.

'I'd better get her home,' said Virgil.

'OK. You carry her to the car. I'll pack up here.'

Thankfully Virgil did as she suggested, but Clara couldn't help but feel as though she'd firmly shut the door on any hope of rekindling a deep and abiding relationship with him for ever. It was clear he knew she'd just brushed him off. That because she hadn't answered his question— hadn't told him that, whether or not she *wanted* to have children, she was physically incapable of doing so—he'd gathered his daughter up and was leaving her. Again.

This time, though, it really was her fault.

Biting her lips, to stop the tears from springing to her eyes as she quickly packed everything into the picnic basket and gathered up the rug whilst trying to ensure Juzzy didn't run away, Clara managed to get things neat and tidy before she dragged in a soothing breath and walked on shaky legs towards Virgil's car.

This would be over soon. He'd bid her a polite farewell, get in his car, take his daughter home, put her to bed and then figure out a way to extract himself from Clara's life. It would happen gradually. He'd see her now and then, but whenever she would suggest getting together he'd tell her how much work he had to do, or say that Rosie needed to spend time with him and—

She stopped the negative hamster wheel from spinning in her mind. She was overthinking things again. She was borrowing trouble. She was selling Virgil short—or at least she hoped she was.

When she reached his car, she placed the basket and rug on the ground as he closed the door, Rosie safely secured inside.

'Did she wake up?' Clara bent to pick up Juzzy, who was starting to weave in and out of her legs, winding the leash into a knot.

'No.'

His one-word answer pierced her heart. Short and to the point.

He collected the picnic basket and rug and stowed them in the boot of his car before jangling the keys from his finger, a sure sign that he was ready to leave her. Well, if this was it—if this was the end of any new beginning for herself and Virgil—she was going to behave with as much dignity as she could muster.

'Thank you for suggesting this.' She gestured to the park, the sky behind them now a lovely mix of pinks, purples and yellows. 'Both Juzzy and I had a lovely time.'

Clara stroked Juzzy's head as she spoke, then jerked her thumb towards her car.

'I'm parked over there, so I'll let you go and see you around the Specialist Centre some time.'

She turned, promising herself she could cry as much as she wanted when she arrived home.

'Clara—wait.' He put his hand on her arm, stopping her from leaving.

She wasn't sure she wanted him to say the words that would bring these wonderful past weeks to an end.

'Could you put Juzzy down on the ground for a moment?'

'Why?'

Virgil quirked an eyebrow at her. 'Because I don't want the dog to get squashed when I kiss you goodnight.'

His perfect lips curved into a half-smile as he took the dog from her arms and placed the Pomeranian on the ground, putting the leash under his shoe to ensure Juzzy remained safely nearby.

A short laugh of disbelief erupted from her before she could stop it. 'Kiss me?'

'Yes.' He chuckled. 'What did you *think* I was going to do?' As he spoke, he reached for her, drawing her close, sliding his arms around her waist. 'A perfect afternoon deserves the perfect ending, and I can think of no better ending than kissing you.'

'But—' Clara frowned, completely thrown by his behaviour. 'But before, when you—'

It didn't matter what she'd been about to say because it appeared Virgil could wait no longer, and he was pressing his lips to hers.

Memories flooded back at his touch—familiarity, acceptance, delight. Virgil was kissing her! Her heart sang with utter excitement. The kiss was soft and questioning, as though he was testing the waters. Slowly—ever so slowly—he moved his lips over hers, tenderly caressing and filling the emptiness she'd tried to lock away for almost six years.

For a brief moment she was certain she could feel raw passion surge through him, but in the next instant his mouth was gently exploring, gently coaxing, to ensure she was right there with him, side by side on this journey into the familiar.

This was Virgil—*her* Virgil—and the love she'd banished all those years ago flooded her like a raging torrent of emotions.

With ardent desire Clara leaned closer to Virgil, thinking how great it felt to feel this way again. She'd thought he would end their budding relationship tonight, but she'd been completely wrong, and it once again proved to her just how much he'd changed. He wasn't her friend from medical school, and he wasn't the focused surgeon eager to make a name for himself. No, the man who was presently making her feel as though she could fly, was someone with wisdom, experience and a clear direction of what he wanted out of life.

She lifted her hands to his head, lacing her fingers in his hair, ensuring his head remained in place so he would continue this sweet, sweet delight upon her senses. Her body was zinging to life, reigniting the spark from so long ago, and their pheromones were combining together to make a heady combination.

Never had she been kissed so tenderly—as though he really did cherish her. It was as though he was trying to show her that she didn't need to be afraid of the electrifying attraction which seemed to hum every time they were near each other. He gently nipped at her lips, causing her eyelids to flutter closed with longing. She wanted to savour every aspect of his kisses, wanted to show him without saying the words just how much she loved being with him.

Eventually it was the need for air which made her tip her head back, unwillingly breaking their connection. As they both dragged air into their lungs, he pressed a smattering of light, feathery kisses to her cheeks, stopping momentarily in the middle to cover her lips with his once more.

'You're addictive,' he murmured against her mouth. 'From the first moment I kissed you until now, you've been like fire in my veins.'

'Mmm...' She kissed him once more before opening her eyes, looking at him through heavy eyelids. 'You make me swoon.' She drew in a slow breath. 'I'm not sure I can stand without help at the moment.'

Virgil smiled and pressed a kiss to the tip of her nose. 'You and me both.' He eased back to look at her. 'Sweetheart, I know there's something bothering you.' His words were as soft and as tender as his kisses. 'I know you too well not to pick up on the signals.'

'Virgil, I—'

'Shh. I won't pry. I'll just continue to show you that you can trust me. I'm here, Clara. For the long haul.'

His tenderness was dangerous, unravelling her tightly wound emotions. Hoping her legs were ready to support her weight, Clara gently eased herself from Virgil's wonderfully strong and protective arms, looking into his hypnotic blue eyes.

'We both need to go our separate ways,' she whispered, unable to believe he'd said he wouldn't pry, that he wanted her to trust him, that he was here for the long haul. A second chance at happiness was at her disposal, and if she tried to explain her swirling emotions now she might make a mess of things. 'You need to get Rosie home.'

'And you need to get Juzzy home.' He kissed her briefly once more, before releasing her from his arms and bending to hand her the dog. 'Just remember one thing for me,' he stated as she took a step backwards. 'This really *is* a new beginning for us, Clara.'

'New beginning…' she repeated, her heart singing with delight. And she ignored that little voice inside which told her it would never last.

CHAPTER NINE

CLARA COULDN'T BELIEVE how well she'd slept last night. 'Kisses from Virgil will do that to you,' she laughingly told her reflection the next day.

As it was Sunday, and neither of them were on call, Virgil phoned her just after midday to see if she was free to spend some more time with him and Rosie.

'We'll just be here—hanging out, playing with toys and avoiding paperwork.'

'Oh? Does Rosie have a lot of paperwork?' she asked, grinning widely as she spoke.

'Stacks. What do you say? Bring Juzzy if you like.'

'I'd really love to, Virgil—'

'But…?' he interrupted, drawing the word out.

'I'm spending time with Arthur and the girls while Maybelle's at work.'

'They can come, too,' Virgil stated. 'I know Rosie would love to play with your nieces.'

'It does sound interesting, but…uh…' She hesitated and Virgil waited expectantly. 'I haven't told Arthur that we're seeing each other again.'

'Ah.' There was silence on the other end of the line for a long moment. 'I take it he isn't my biggest fan?'

'Not really, no.'

'That's understandable. I did break his sister's heart.'

'I was going to tell him this afternoon. Let him know how much you've changed…that things are different this time.'

'At least he allowed his daughters to come and enjoy a play date with Rosie.'

'He's fine with you living and working here. And he's fine with his daughters playing with your daughter.'

'But he's not fine when it comes to you and me together?'

'Something like that. I *will* talk to him, Virgil. Today.'

'It's all right, Clara. Take your time.'

Although his impatience was beginning to surge, he reminded himself that he had the rest of his life to show Clara—and the rest of her family—that he was a changed man, that he adored her and that his intentions were extremely honourable.

He spoke to Clara for a few more minutes, then rang off and leaned back in his chair. He shouldn't have been surprised that Clara's brother wasn't his biggest fan, and it was good that Arthur was still looking out for his sister.

Before arriving back in Loggeen, the last time he'd seen Arthur Lewis had been the night before his early flight to Montreal. Arthur had turned up at Virgil's apartment, giving him an earful.

'She loves you!' Arthur had stated. 'And this is how you treat her?'

'It's my *career*, Arthur. I thought at least *you'd* understand. You're chasing your own career dreams.'

'Not overseas. I'm not running away when the going gets tough.'

'What? I'm not running away.'

'Clara told me that you had plans to get married and start a family. She wants that with you.'

'I never asked her to marry me.'

That revelation had brought Arthur up short. 'But Clara said—'

'We've discussed it on occasions, but there have been no firm plans made. I can't make firm plans until I've sorted out my career. This opportunity in Montreal is a once-in-a-lifetime sort of deal and I'm not going to turn it down. Not for you. Not for Clara. Not for anyone.'

'Your career isn't your *life*, Virgil.'

'Yes, it is.'

'No. Your career is just your job. It's not where you live.' Arthur had pointed to his heart. 'Jobs will come and go, but do you know how difficult it is to find the love of a woman who adores you the way Clara does? When you have your big successes in your career, who are you going to share them with? When you've have a bad day at work, who's going to support you?'

Arthur's words had made him stop, had made him ponder those questions for a moment or two, but then he'd shaken his head. 'It's too late to think like that. I've made my decision. My flight leaves in ten hours' time and I still have packing to do.'

He'd indicated the front door to his apartment.

'You'd better go.'

'So that's it? You're just going to *leave* her?'

'She'll be fine. She's a smart, intelligent woman.'

'Yeah. She is.' Arthur had walked to the door, wrenching it open. 'And *you're* the fool who let her go.'

And what a fool he'd been. He didn't blame Arthur for being over-protective of Clara. He was glad she had a family who loved and supported her, and he knew that if he was to stand any chance with Clara in the future, he needed to make amends with Arthur, too. Family was important. Rosie had taught him that. For now he would follow Clara's lead where Arthur was concerned, trusting her to guide him.

* * *

Later that evening Virgil received a phone call from the ED, calling him in.

'There's been a bad accident. Retrieval teams are preparing,' the nurse told him.

Thankfully, Rosie was already in bed, and after quickly telling Gwenda he was heading to the hospital Virgil walked briskly to his car. If the retrieval teams were getting ready to go out, there was a high probability that Clara was leading the team.

When he arrived at the hospital it was to find it a hive of activity. He stood still for one long moment, scanning the room until he found her. She was standing at the nurses' desk, talking to Arthur and Larissa, one of the ED nurses.

He headed towards them and upon greeting them, received a normal 'Hello', from Larissa; a growl accompanied by a frown from Arthur, and a subdued but happy, 'Hello, thank goodness you could make it,' from Clara. It wasn't so much what she said, but the softening of her gaze as it came to rest on him. It was a nice sensation to have.

'What's the situation?'

'Briefing in five minutes,' she told him. 'Why don't you get changed into retrieval overalls?' She indicated her bright orange jumpsuit, covered with pockets and reflective tape here and there. 'Meet us in the briefing room?'

'Good.' He nodded and left to do as instructed.

How was it possible she could make those clothes look as though they were the latest fashion? The woman was amazing.

She ran a successful and very busy general practice, and he knew she was up to date with her paperwork as he'd received reports on Michelle and also Linda and Henry Santorino, who had been discharged and were doing well. She worked two shifts per month at the hospital's Emergency Department and led the retrieval teams, helped out with her nieces and was well liked by everyone she met. Was it any wonder he was completely and utterly smitten with her?

He knew there was something deep that was troubling her, but he had to trust her to tell him when she was ready. He wouldn't push. He wouldn't pry—no matter how badly he wanted to know why she would sometimes sit and stare at nothing, tears springing to her eyes. Or why she would abruptly change the subject or distract him from discussing things further.

When he entered the briefing room, it was to find it almost full to bursting. Clara was standing at the front of the room, and as soon as she saw him enter she started to speak. Had she been waiting for him? Just as well he hadn't dilly-dallied.

'Right, listen up.'

She spoke to all the people who were in the small briefing room, some of them already in their bright orange retrieval overalls and others who were just arriving. Virgil stood near the back. As a general surgeon, the best place for him to be would be here at the hospital, waiting for the casualties to be brought to Theatre, but after reading the particulars of this accident, Clara knew she needed him at the crash site.

'There are two people trapped in a car, and the car has gone over an embankment on the road heading to the coast.' Clara spoke clearly. 'One male, one female in the car. The Country Fire Service and police are in attendance. The car has rolled several times, so we can expect head injuries, seatbelt injuries and a plethora of internal injuries.'

She glanced towards Virgil as she spoke.

'You all know your strengths—work to them. Let's work as a team and attend to our patients. Go and grab your gear. Meet out at the ambulances in five minutes.'

With that, she dismissed everyone and people scattered to do their jobs.

Virgil was the only one left. 'You sounded like a coach. What's your strategy?'

'Pumping everyone up. Adrenaline. We have no idea what we're going to find and, quite frankly, Virgil, sometimes even the less gory scenes can still turn my stomach. Getting pumped up and preparing our minds mentally for what we'll find is a big issue. It helps us cope.' She crossed her arms and looked at him. 'How long is it since you've been out with a retrieval team, rather than just judging them at competitions?'

'Too long to remember,' Virgil answered with a shake of his head.

'Well, then, Dr Arterton.' Clara grinned up at him and winked. 'You might just learn something new.'

'Oh—my—goodness.' Clara said each word slowly as she straightened from looking over the side of the mountain. 'Is the car stable?'

The policeman, who had been the first at the accident site, nodded. 'We've managed to get a cable around the front axle, which will hold the front of the car quite firmly. Other cables have been attached to the driver's side and the rear of the car is wedged firmly into the ground.' He held out his hand to her and shook it briefly. 'I'm Senior Sergeant Edelstein and I'll be in charge up here.'

'Dr Clara Lewis. I'll be in charge of things down there.' She inclined her head to indicate the accident site.

The road had been closed off and the area was swarming with emergency personnel. Clara looked again at the car that was lit by two huge floodlamps that the Country Fire Service had set up.

The car had rolled a number of times and had finally come to rest on its side—passenger side down. As the policeman had informed her, the rear of the car had dug itself into the ground while the front was resting on an old gum tree.

As the CFS personnel had managed to secure some cables around the car, in case the tree branches gave way, the car would be suspended horizontally out from the side of the mountain. At least that was what they'd told her would happen.

Clara could feel her heart begin to pound in her ears. She'd told Virgil it was adrenaline that got them through these situations, and she realised she was going to need a heck of a lot to get through this one.

'What's the plan, Clara?' asked Geoff, her retrieval team buddy.

The rest of the team gathered around to hear what she had to say. Virgil was listening intently too. All of them were suited up with abseiling harnesses and ropes, ready to scale down the mountain to the accident site.

'The CFS have removed what was left of the front windscreen, which will make our job a little easier. They recommend getting the female passenger out first, and then the driver. He's being held in by his seatbelt and the steering wheel, so once we remove those obstacles gravity will naturally pull him downwards. If the passenger is out of the way we'll have more room to manoeuvre. These CFS guys know what they're talking about and have already been down several times so we'll heed their advice.'

Everyone nodded and Clara continued.

'We need to have as little contact with the car as possible. They've said those cables will hold, but I don't want any unnecessary risks taken. If the danger is too great then we don't take the risk. Understood?'

'Yes,' everyone answered.

'Virgil, you go on the passenger side with the stretcher. You'll need to get down lower than the car, so that when

Geoff and I lower her out she can go straight down on to the stretcher rather than being winched upwards.

'Geoff, you'll be with me, assisting with what I'll need.' She turned to one of the retrieval nurses. 'Amelia, get an area set up here, so when Virgil comes up with the female passenger everything he'll need will be ready.'

'On it,' Amelia stated.

'There has been no sign of consciousness yet, but when the CFS team checked, both patients were alive, their airways were clear and breathing was not compromised. We'll stabilise the injuries as best we can and then secure the harness around her. Once she's ready, we move her out. We'll have had a chance to assess the other patient, but will probably need the foot pedals and steering wheel to be cut away before we can remove him.'

She took a deep breath, knowing she needed to keep a cool, clear head. She couldn't look at Virgil too much because the last time she'd glanced his way, she'd seen a huge furrow on his brow—one of concern, not just for the patients, but for her as well. She couldn't think about that now. It was imperative she take things step by step and keep calm.

'Everyone knows their jobs. Let's do this.'

She had the CFS re-check her harness before she abseiled closer to the vehicle. The entire retrieval team were wearing headphone sets so they could easily talk to each other, as well as communicate with the rest of the emergency crew up top.

'To your right. Good. Now, slowly.'

Virgil was already in position, below and off to the side of the car. From where he hung, secured by his ropes, he could see everything.

'Geoff, stop your descent so Clara can get into position,' Virgil stated through his headset. 'Clara, a little more to your right.'

Clara was just passing the rear of the car, which was wedged into the ground. *Unbelievable*, she thought but kept her focus firmly on her work. As the car was still balancing on the strong gum tree branches, Clara needed Virgil's guidance to assist her through the maze.

'Watch that branch on your right. Good. Carefully find your way through.' Virgil's deep voice was clear and calm and she drew strength from it. 'Good,' he encouraged her as she moved just below the smashed front windscreen.

Securely held, Clara was ready to work.

The driver was hanging by his seatbelt, the steering wheel effectively jamming him firmly in place. The woman was pressed against the passenger window, her own seatbelt holding her securely. Thank goodness both had been wearing seatbelts, Clara thought, otherwise their services wouldn't have been required at all.

'Thanks, Virgil. Talk Geoff down while I take a look around.'

The light on her helmet illuminated the area, but she reached into her top pocket for a small medical torch. After taking the woman's pulse, which was faint, Clara quickly checked the pupils.

'Both pupils are constricting. Pulse is faint but present. There's a lot of blood,' Clara reported.

The woman was beginning to moan and Clara instantly tried to calm her.

'You're going to be fine. Help is here. I'm Clara—a doctor.' Clara's voice was firm but gentle.

'I feel…weak…' The woman's voice was a broken whisper.

'What's your name?' Clara asked as she waited for Geoff to get into position.

'Hmm…? G-Gale,' the woman answered after a moment.

'And your friend? What's his name?' Clara asked.

It looked as though Gale was ready to pass out again, but before she did she said softly, 'Dan.'

'Virgil, I'm going to need the largest compression bandage you have. I'll also need a neck brace to keep her head stable. Our patients' names are Gale and Dan. Gale has severe lacerations to the abdomen. Extensive bleeding. I couldn't even begin to guess what's been ruptured. It looks as though something has gashed her right across her stomach. Query fractured pelvis.'

Clara was hanging right beside the windscreen, almost parallel with it, and was therefore able to reach around to treat Gale's injuries.

'What about Dan?' Virgil asked as he manoeuvred himself into position to help.

'I can't get to him until we have Gale safely out of the way. I don't want to risk scrambling over the bonnet to check him out. The entire centre of gravity of the car would change.' She shook her head. 'He's unconscious at the moment, so until the situation changes we'll leave it at that.'

'Good call.'

Virgil continued to assist Clara as they treated Gale's injuries as best they could, needing to stabilise her before they could transfer her to the stretcher. When they were ready, Clara contacted Senior Sergeant Edelstein via her headset.

'Edelstein here,' the police sergeant at the top of the mountain replied tersely.

'Gale's medical harness is attached to the ropes. Have your team standing by. We're almost ready to move the patient to the stretcher below.'

'Will do.'

'Virgil, you'll need to come closer to help me support Gale. We need to keep her as horizontal as we possibly can. Sergeant Edelstein, get ready with the winch on the patient's ropes.'

'Standing by for your signal, Dr Lewis,' the police sergeant reported.

'Gale,' said Clara softly. 'We're going to move you now.'

Although Clara had administered pain relief, she hoped her patient remained unconscious until she was safely at the top.

'On three…' She waited for a moment while Virgil and Geoff came into position, so they could achieve this with as little fuss as possible. 'One. Two.' She held her breath and offered up a silent prayer. 'Three!'

The winch started moving and slowly Gale was hoisted from the car and lowered, through careful and meticulous instruction from Clara, to the waiting stretcher. Once she was there, Virgil's job began as he ensured Gale's safety and double-checked her bandages.

'All clear, Clara,' he reported. 'She's ready to go to the top.'

'Right. Sergeant Edelstein, the stretcher is ready, so start easing her up slowly. Virgil, you accompany Gale while Geoff and I check Dan's situation.'

Soon Gale was halfway up the mountain, with Virgil rising steadily beside her.

'Geoff, I'd like to take a closer look at Dan and check him out.'

'Be careful, Clara.'

'I always am, mate.' She turned and smiled at the RN. 'Thankfully the car didn't shift when we moved Gale, and as I'm roughly the same size I should be fine.'

Gingerly, Clara pulled herself slightly up on her rope, so her feet were hanging level with the car's open windscreen. Keeping her body as still as possible, she began to lower herself through the opening and into the spot Gale had recently vacated.

'I'm in.' She exhaled slowly with relief.

Stretching upwards, Clara pressed two fingers to Dan's

carotid pulse and found that it was slightly stronger than Gale's had been. She reported her findings into her head-set. 'Pupils are constricting.'

Clara took a better look at the way Dan was jammed in and sighed resignedly.

'The steering wheel is all but sitting in his pelvis and his legs are well and truly jammed. Paraplegia would be my guess, but I sincerely hope I'm wrong. Sergeant Edel-stein, I suggest we come up and the CFS crews come down to cut Dan free.'

'Roger that.'

Once she and Geoff were at the top, she headed over to where Virgil was pulling off a pair of bloodied gloves. 'How is she?'

'Almost everything is ruptured,' Virgil told Clara as Gale's stretcher was transferred to the ambulance. 'I found small splinters of wood. I'd say that a roadside fence pal-ing smashed through the windscreen as the car rolled and gashed Gale's abdomen.'

'Get to the hospital and do what you do best, Dr Arterton. Save a life.'

Clara held his gaze for a long moment before he climbed into the back of the ambulance. Virgil took the opportu-nity to put his hand on her arm, his eyes filled with fear and concern.

'You be careful when you go back down. Don't get into the vehicle. It's too unstable.'

'I'll make sure the CFS crews recheck the cables before I head down,' she stated.

'But—' He stopped, hesitating over whether or not to continue voicing his concerns. After staring into her eyes for a moment, he leaned forward and pressed a kiss to her lips. '*Please* be careful.'

Clara's heart fused with love for him. She could see he didn't want her going down, that he was concerned for her own safety, but he knew she had a job to do and he appreciated her skills.

She nodded, unable to find the words to reassure him as her throat had constricted with love for him.

CHAPTER TEN

CLARA AND THE rest of the retrieval team had extracted Dan from the car and got him back to the hospital. There had been one or two complications but they'd managed to prevail in the end. She checked with the theatre clerk and found that Virgil was still in Theatre with Gale. She handed over Dan's care to the orthopaedic registrar, then sat down to complete her reports, all the while just wanting to go home and sleep.

She was just finishing up the final report when Virgil sauntered towards her, still in scrubs and looking utterly exhausted. 'How's Gale?'

'Stable in Recovery. She'll need further surgery, but for now I can't do much more. I'm just waiting for the orthopaedic guys to call me in to do my bit on Dan.'

'He was in a bad way when we got him out, but I've seen worse and people have lived.'

'Like you?' Virgil sat beside her, wheeling his chair as close as possible, then leaning forward and pressing a brief kiss on her lips. 'I'm so glad you're OK.'

Clara pursed her lips and nodded, not wanting to talk about her accident, not wanting to open those flood doors on emotion, pain and anguish.

'You *are* OK, aren't you?' Virgil prompted when she didn't say anything.

'Yeah, I'm good.' She returned her attention to the computer.

'It's just that after seeing Gale's injuries, and still waiting to comprehend how bad Dan's are, it's made me realise I really don't know all that much about your accident except that you sustained a pelvic fracture and were in hospital and rehab for the better part of a year. For you to be incapacitated for such a long time can only mean your injuries really were extensive.'

Clara saved her work on the computer, then turned to face him, needing to ensure her professional mask was in place before she spoke. 'Yes, it was bad. No, I don't want to discuss it—especially not now.' She could feel her skin starting to get clammy and rubbed her hands together to combat it.

'Did tonight's retrieval bring back memories?'

'Retrievals always bring it back—especially when the team and I are trying to save a patient's life and I'm harnessed in and the only way to free the patient is to climb into the wreckage.'

'You went back in? I asked you not to.' Virgil straightened up and spread his arms wide.

'It was a judgement call. I discussed it with my team. Everyone was safe, and when the car shifted, all I sustained was a bruise on my arm—for which I've just finished filling out an incident report.'

'It *shifted*! Clara!' He stood and glared down at her. 'You could have been killed.'

'But I wasn't. Calm down.' She glanced around the ED and noticed that some of the staff were looking their way. 'Shh. You're making a scene and disturbing the patients.'

Virgil shoved his hands into his pockets and looked at the ground, counting to ten. She'd seen him in this mood several times in the past, and even though she felt highly self-conscious right now, thanks to his outburst, she was impressed with the way he was really controlling that temper of his.

'Let me see your arm.'

'It's fine.'

'Please?'

Rolling her eyes, she showed him the enormous bruise on her upper arm, noting that it was already changing colour, dark purples starting to appear. 'There. Satisfied?'

The phone on the desk rang and Clara instantly snatched it up, eager to look away from Virgil's concerned eyes. 'Emergency Department.' She glanced across at Virgil. 'Yes, he's here. I'll tell him.' She hung up the receiver.

'Theatre?'

She nodded. 'Go work your magic and help save Dan's life.'

She smiled encouragingly but knew it wasn't a heartfelt smile. The strain of the night was starting to take its toll and all she wanted was to head home, take a shower and crawl into bed.

Virgil stood where he was, watching her closely. 'It'll probably be time for breakfast when I get out of Theatre. Mind if I pop round?'

'If you want to check up on me, then just say so.' She lifted her chin with defiance, calling his bluff.

'OK, then. I want to check up on you, to make sure you're all right, and that you don't have any physical or emotional repercussions from tonight's retrieval.'

'You don't have to, Virgil. I'm fi—'

'I want to, and I'm going to. I'll be round when I'm out of Theatre. Until then, try and get some sleep.' He leaned forward and pressed a concerned kiss to her lips. 'I love you, Clara.'

With that, he turned on his heel and headed off to do his job.

* * *

She was driving along. She was in a car and she didn't feel sick. This was a good thing. Wasn't it? But, wait, things around her were changing. She was now standing in the middle of Melbourne General's cafeteria and everyone was pointing and laughing at her.

'He left you.'

'He broke your heart and he doesn't care about you.'

'You'll never find love.'

Clara looked around at the people, some dressed in scrubs, some wearing white coats, some with stethoscopes around their necks.

'Why are you saying this?' she asked, but the only answer she received was a roaring round of people laughing.

Their laughing changed to shrieking, and then it wasn't laughter. It was the sound of tyres squealing on the bitumen road. It was the sound of crunching metal.

She was being spun around and around and around. She was back in the car, trying to clutch the steering wheel, trying to focus on the song on the radio, but the warbling noise made no sense. Nothing made any sense. Pain pierced her legs and metal seemed to fold in around her.

Clara tried to drag in a breath, tried to fill her lungs with air so she could scream, so she could alert the authorities to let them know that she'd been hurt. Where was the ambulance? Where were the doctors?

'Code Blue. Code Blue,' she kept trying to say, but her lungs refused to fill with air and she was unable to speak.

Gasping for breath, she felt a pulse of dread shoot through her, twisting her neck into a very uncomfortable angle.

She tried to look around her, but all she could see was the outside of the car she was in, hurtling through the darkened streets like a small ball in a pinball machine. The car went one way and hit a lamp post, the impact almost fold-ing the metal giant in two. Then the car hurtled back the other way, smashing into some parked cars.

Clara blinked. She was still inside the car, but the large spacious inside cabin was now reduced to the side of a small cube, as though the car had been put through one of those giant compactors used in scrap metal yards. She needed to contort herself if she was going to fit, if she was going to survive this ordeal.

But did she want to survive?

Images of Virgil swam into her vision and once again she was back in the hospital cafeteria, with people pointing and laughing at her, telling her she'd never find true love ever again.

He'd left her.

He'd told her she wasn't important in his life, that his career would come first and he'd left her.

It was clear by his actions that she hadn't meant as much to him as he'd meant to her.

Virgil had been her one true love. Her friend for such a long time, her confidant, her study support. Now he wasn't here. He'd left her and he wouldn't be able to help her contort herself enough to fit into the tiny space which was now left inside the car.

Darkness threatened to engulf her—darkness at being all alone. She felt as though she were suspended in mid-air, in a sort of sling, trying to reach out to the people around her, trying to attract their attention, but no one seemed to be hearing her cries for help.

'It's because their careers are more important than you.'

Virgil's words swam into her mind and she looked around for him.

'Virgil? Virgil?'

She tried to call, but once again her lungs refused to fill with air and wouldn't co-operate with her vocal cords in making any sort of noise.

Why couldn't he hear her? Why had he left her? Why hadn't he loved her?

The next thing she knew she was sitting in a hospital bed, unable to move her lower limbs. Her pelvis was fractured in several places, her legs were broken, her toes crushed. Doctors were talking to her, telling her she'd been in Theatre for a long time and would still need several more operations, but they were hopeful she'd walk again.

'Unfortunately,' her doctors were saying, 'there was also a lot of damage to your internal organs. Your bladder was ruptured and your womb was damaged beyond repair.'

Damaged beyond repair.

They wanted to remove it, or they had removed it, or something else had happened. But her womb was gone. The bladder was fixed but she'd have to retrain it. One of her kidneys had also been damaged, but they were hopeful about that, too.

Clara looked behind the doctors to see her father holding her mother close, her mother weeping. Arthur stood next to his parents, patting his mother on the back, then he shifted and was standing next to the surgeons, nodding sadly and reading her charts as though he needed to re-check the information for himself.

Then everyone disappeared and she was left there. In traction. Unable to move. Suspended. Hanging there like a puppet whose strings were all tangled and its limbs in a mess.

She closed her eyes, wanting to have it all stop. She wanted it to stop. She wanted her world to just—*stop*!

Clara sat bolt upright in bed, her body bathed in sweat and trembling with fear. Gasping for air, she clutched a hand to her chest and stared unseeingly at her surroundings. The pictures on the wall. The light fixture on the ceiling. She was in her bedroom. She was safe. She was OK.

Slowly, she managed to calm her breathing as she climbed from the sheets and walked out into the kitchen to get a cool glass of water. The clock indicated it was almost six a.m. Sitting down at her kitchen table, she concentrated on deep breathing exercises. It had been years since she'd had a terrible nightmare about her car accident, but perhaps she shouldn't be surprised, considering the retrieval she'd just been through.

Clara had been trapped for almost seven hours before they'd finally managed to cut her free and transfer her to the Melbourne General Hospital emergency department—*her* department, at the place where she worked. Thankfully, the specialists had taken great care of her, but being a patient in the hospital where she had trained and worked had been an eye-opening experience.

Virgil had gone. Left her for his career. He'd left her and gone to start a new life for himself in Canada.

'Should I call him? Tell him?' Arthur had asked as he'd sat by her hospital bed in the intensive care unit.

Clara had been hooked up to several machines to monitor her vital signs, and she'd been in traction after several hours of surgery. Arthur, being the wonderful sibling he was, had told her she looked as though she'd gone several rounds against a champion boxer—and won!

Clara hadn't been sure she wanted Virgil knowing anything about her life now. *He* was the one who had chosen to leave, who had betrayed her. The real question which had nestled deep within her heart had been would he come back to be with her if he *did* know? Clara had been through too much heartbreak to risk him not bothering to return.

'Why?'

Her voice had been raspy and dry. Arthur had immediately given her a spoonful of ice chips.

'He clearly doesn't love me. If he did, he would have accepted me for who I am.'

To speak the words out loud had nearly caused as much emotional damage as the accident had caused physical damage.

Clara had had to come to terms with a lot in those first few days—especially the news that her womb and one of her ovaries had been removed.

'I'll never be able to have children, Mum,' Clara had wailed, and together she and her mother had wept, their tears somehow binding them closer together.

Her parents and Arthur had been wonderful, caring for her while she'd been an inpatient in hospital and looking after her life outside the hospital.

'The doctors say you're going to need a lot of rehabilitation once all your surgeries are done,' her father had said. 'And...er...' He'd looked across at her mother, who had nodded encouragingly. 'We wanted you to come and live with us when you get out.'

It was then that Clara had realised she was still paying rent on an empty apartment, and although she'd had accident insurance, there was only so far that would stretch. Her parents had helped her make some difficult decisions—namely breaking her lease and putting her furniture and belongings into storage.

Clara had been cut off from the outside world. Her new world had consisted of one medical appointment after another. Doctors, lawyers, physiotherapists, dieticians, psychologists—the list had gone on and on, and once Clara had been finally released from the rehabilitation hospital, nearly eight months later, she had gone home with her parents.

Her family had been incredible, and the accident had most definitely brought them all closer together.

'You're our miracle girl,' her mother had told Clara once. 'As hard as this year has been, you weren't taken from us, darling. That's all I care about.'

Eventually Clara had been able to think about working again, and Arthur had found her this apartment. Her parents had been more than happy to have her move out knowing her big brother was just downstairs.

Now, as she sat at the table, Clara sipped the cool water and shoved her hands through her hair, surprised to find she'd been perspiring. Given she often repressed a lot of those old emotions about that traumatic time of her life, and after tonight's emergency retrieval, was it any wonder her subconscious had burst open and given her the nightmare of the year?

Rising, Clara went to the cupboard where she stored her medical kit and took some paracetamol to help with the ache pounding in her head. No sooner had she swallowed them than she heard a soft knocking at her front door. Glancing down at her attire of comfortable pyjamas, and deciding she was decent enough for company, she opened the door.

'Hi.'

'Hi,' Virgil responded, and when she stepped back to allow him entry, he came in.

Clara shut the door behind him and noticed he was looking around the room, taking in the decor of her apartment.

'Nice place. Where's Juzzy?'

'Asleep on my bed.' She frowned. 'I think… Or she might be in her basket. Either way, it's too early for that princess to be out of bed.'

Virgil smiled, but it didn't last long as he studied her. 'How are you feeling?'

'OK.'

He glanced behind her, noticing the box of paracetamol and the half-drunk glass of water.

'Really?'

Without another word, he covered the distance between

them and gathered her into his arms as though needing to share her pain.

'Is the headache bad?'

'It's just a mild one.'

'Liar.'

Her answer was to shrug one shoulder.

'Tonight's accident brought all your memories back, didn't it?' he asked softly. He eased back and looked deeply into her eyes before scanning her face. 'Have you had a nightmare?'

Clara nodded.

'Then why do you put yourself through doing retrievals if it brings back horrible memories?'

'Because I remember the people who were there when *I* was being cut out of the car.'

'You were cut out of the car!'

She nodded. 'A reckless drunk driver smashed into me. My car rolled, smashing its way through the streets, collecting a lamp-post and a few other cars on its way. I was trapped for seven hours, and during that time those people in the retrieval team were my lifeline. There were so many times when I really couldn't be bothered to fight. I wanted to *die*, Virgil.'

'Don't say that,' he implored.

'It's true.' She looked down at where his hand was still on top of hers, his fingers intertwined with her own. 'The accident happened two weeks after you left. When the hospital grapevine was working overtime with gossip about the way you'd left me—'

'Clara, I'm sorry.'

'I was crying non-stop, highly emotional, trying not to snap at the people around me and just wanting to finish my contract at the hospital and to be anywhere except where I was.'

Clara stopped, tears instantly springing to her eyes.

'I wanted to die that night, Virgil. I wanted it all to be over and done with. No more pain. No more problems. No more gossip. No more having to live my life without you.'

'Don't—just *don't*.'

She could hear the distraught sound of his voice but she continued. 'My body was as broken as my heart, and in a twisted, strange way it made me feel better. A lot of people can't see a broken heart, and I was able to hide mine—to lock it away while I focused on healing my body, going through surgery and then rehabilitation.'

Tears were slowly rolling down Clara's cheeks as she spoke, and when she'd finished Virgil gently wiped them away.

Leaning over, he claimed her lips, the touch tender and gentle. 'I'm sorry I broke your heart. I'm *so* sorry, Clara. If I had a time machine and could go back and slap some sense into my younger self, then I would. I would do that in a heartbeat. But I can't.'

He sniffed.

'All we can do now is to take what we've managed to salvage from the past and think of the fantastic things we've been sharing these past few weeks. We need to move forward with our lives.'

As he spoke Virgil started to yawn, and although he tried to hide it, it was to no avail.

'We need sleep.' Clara stood, but kept holding his hand. 'Come on.'

'Clara, if you're feeling amorous,' he stated as she led him towards the bedroom, switching off the lights as she went, 'you've chosen a terrible time, because I am *exhausted*.'

'Shh. I'm too tired and so are you. Just hold me, Virgil,' she whispered as the darkness of the room settled over them. 'Like you used to. Safe and secure. That's what I need tonight.'

'Your wish is my command,' he told her.

Clara climbed beneath the covers and waited for Virgil to join her. He kept his trousers on and she was grateful. He really did understand that, for tonight, all she needed was his arms, comforting and holding her. Washing away the past and the nightmares that lived there.

Snuggling deeper under the covers, Clara closed her eyes. Felt the warmth of Virgil's chest beneath her ear as she rested her head there, listening to his heart beating with its regular healthy rhythm.

This was where she truly belonged. This was where nothing bad could ever touch her. With Virgil at her side, Clara felt as though she could conquer the world.

But could she conquer the world if Virgil really knew all about her—warts and all?

CHAPTER ELEVEN

CLARA STIRRED LAZILY, slowly waking from the best sleep she could ever remember having. As she lay there with her eyes shut, trying to remember what day of the week it was, memories of the previous night came flooding back. The stress of the difficult retrieval, the nightmare as she'd relived her own accident, the way Virgil had comforted and supported her.

The last memory made her smile and she reached out a hand to the pillow beside her, expecting to touch his face or feel his body beside hers, but he wasn't there. Opening her eyes, she raised herself up onto her elbows. Whilst the covers were a little crumpled, and whilst she could most definitely smell his enticing scent on the sheets next to her, there was no sign of Virgil.

It was then she glanced at the clock and nearly levitated off the mattress.

'Half past twelve!'

She had a busy Monday morning clinic to attend to!

Clara threw back the covers and scrambled out. 'Virgil?' she called as she softly padded out to the kitchen. No answer. 'Virgil?' she called again, a little louder this time. Still no reply.

A quick tour of her apartment confirmed that Virgil wasn't anywhere to be found.

She checked her phone to see if he'd left her a message, and sure enough there was one text. It simply said:

You deserve a sleep-in. Your patients have been taken care of, so rest. Talk soon.

There were no little kisses, no emojis attached to the message. At the thought of Virgil sending her a message with emojis attached she grinned, because he really wasn't an emoji type of guy.

She quickly called the clinic, wondering if Jane had spent the better part of the morning cancelling her patients. When Jane answered, it was with a bright and easy air.

'Jane. It's Clara. I'm so sorry I didn't turn up this morning, but with the retrieval last night and—'

'Don't sweat it,' Jane remarked. 'Between Virgil and Arthur, all your patients have been seen. Mrs Holden was especially pleased to see the dashing Dr Arterton. She called him a "dish". Is that a compliment?'

'Virgil *and* Arthur saw my patients this morning?'

'Yep. Virgil did the first few hours and Arthur's just finishing off now.'

'But Arthur's supposed to be at the hospital!'

'Maybelle's covering for him there.' Jane chuckled. 'It's OK, Clara. We've all got your back and...well—' she giggled '—when Virgil gives you that smile and looks at you with those gorgeous blue eyes of his, how can you possibly say no!'

'Gosh, I hope he didn't use that trick on Arthur,' Clara mumbled, still confused as to how Virgil had managed to get Arthur to agree.

She rang off and decided that as her afternoon clinic didn't start for another hour, she could at least have some breakfast. As she made herself some coffee and patted her dog, she pondered Arthur's reaction to Virgil's request.

When Clara had told her brother that she was seeing Virgil again, Arthur had been cautiously protective but not entirely surprised.

'I've been watching him around the hospital this past month—watching how he is with his patients, with the staff—and I have to say he has changed from the egocentric man of the past.'

'So you're OK with me seeing him?'

'Clara, you're a grown woman. You can make your own decisions.'

'But do you think it's a mistake?'

Arthur had hugged her close. 'Whether it is or not, I think you owe it to the two of you to find out.' He'd paused, then asked, 'Does he know about the accident?'

'He knows.'

'And about the extent of your injuries? That you can't carry a child?'

'Er...no.'

Arthur had let her go, but given her his best 'brother knows best' stare. 'You need to tell him, Clara. If you *are* going to end up together, he deserves to know.'

'I know, I know. I will—and soon.'

And yet as she finished her coffee and headed to her room to get dressed, she realised she still hadn't had that conversation with Virgil. After this morning, when he'd come by and stayed with her, holding her, letting her sleep, and then organising to cover her clinic...

She clutched her hands to her chest and sighed. It was the most romantic thing he'd ever done for her. She knew she owed him the truth—that if they were going to have any future together he needed to be aware that she could never give him a child.

With the way he loved Rosie, plus the few times he'd raised the topic of children, she instinctively knew he wanted more—and she couldn't give him any. Would that

matter? Would he still want to be with her? He'd told her
last night, before she'd left to come home, that he loved
her. Why had he said that? All it had done was put more
pressure on her. And whilst her exhausted heart had soared
with happiness at the declaration, she'd also felt a band beginning to constrict around her heart.

The only way forward was to face the inevitable, and
the sooner she did that, the sooner she would know where
she stood.

She had to tell Virgil, and soon.

After her afternoon clinic had been completed, Clara
headed over to the hospital for a debrief with the rest of
the retrieval team from last night's accident. Before the
debriefing, Clara went to check on Dan and Gale, and
was pleased to discover that they were both off the criti-
cal list. Throughout the debriefing she found it difficult
to keep her concentration on what she and the other emergency officials were saying, given that Virgil was standing close by her.

'You've got it bad,' her brother whispered in her ear
once the briefing was done.

Virgil was chatting with Geoff on the other side of the
room and Clara was simply standing there, watching him.
Arthur's comments brought her back to reality. Several of
the other staff members were heading out of the room, and
soon it was just herself and Arthur, with Virgil and Geoff
deep in discussion on the other side of the room.

'What?' She turned her back to Virgil and focused her
attention on Arthur.

'Virgil. You really are in love with him.' It was a statement and Arthur shrugged a shoulder. 'Happens to the
best of us.'

'You've changed your tune. You were telling me to be
careful and—'

'And I still am, but I have to say I was very intrigued earlier this morning, when I opened my front door, to find him standing there asking me to help him cover your clinic so you could rest.' Arthur gave her a concerned look. 'He mentioned you'd had bad dreams about your accident. Are you OK?'

'Yeah. Often happens after car accident retrievals.'

'I know.' Arthur hugged her close for a moment. 'And where Virgil is concerned, I have to say I'm impressed. He really does love you, Clara.'

'Yeah?'

'And he wants to marry you.'

'Wait. What? How do you know?'

'Because when I asked him what his intentions were towards you, that's what he told me.'

Her eyes widened. 'He did?' Then her gaze turned worried. 'You didn't tell him about—?'

'No. That's your job. But whatever happens…'

He kissed her forehead, leaving the rest of the sentence unspoken because she knew what he was talking about. He would always be there for her, no matter what.

'Anyway, I'd best get back to work. Lots of paperwork to fill in and rosters to write. You still OK with your two shifts per month on a Saturday night?'

'Sure am, bro.'

'Good. That means you're working this Saturday and I get the night off to spend with my family.'

With that, Arthur headed out of the room. Clara turned to gather up her reports, but when she turned back it was to find Virgil walking towards her, grinning.

'Hi, there,' he stated. 'Did you have a nice sleep-in?'

'I did. I sent you a text, conveying my thanks, but I'll say it in person, too. Thank you for organising my clinic and my patients and people to help. I appreciate it.'

'Your family love you…as do I.'

'Virgil—' She stopped and looked down at the floor, unsure what to do or say next, because every time he said that he loved her, she felt the most glorious warmth and happiness wash over her before the hefty weight of guilt settled on her shoulders.

'Too soon? I can stop saying it.'

'No—it's not that. It's—' She glanced around the room, and although they were the last two people there she knew this wasn't the place to tell him what she needed to say. 'I need to talk to you.'

He was instantly concerned. 'Are you all right?'

'Yeah. I just need to share some things with you.'

'If you're not ready, I don't want to pry, Clara. You need to be ready.'

'I am.' She nodded for emphasis.

He smiled at her words and gazed into her eyes as though she'd just given him the moon. She hoped he still felt like that after he'd heard what she had to say.

'Do you have time now, or are you expected home for dinner? I wouldn't want you to miss putting Rosie to bed.'

'I was going to check on my patients in the ward, then head home. You could join me? Help me put Rosie to bed?'

'OK. Sounds good.'

His smile increased as he headed out of the room, leaving her clutching her reports to her chest and hoping against hope that she was doing the right thing.

Of *course* it was the right thing. If she was going to forge any sort of future with him, be able to put her trust in him once again, then she needed to address the past.

With a thread of determination running through her, Clara marched towards her future with her head held high and a heart full of hope.

When Virgil pulled into his driveway, his spirits were soaring. There was a spring in his step as he collected his briefcase and the flowers he'd stopped to buy on the way home. Clara was coming over to tell him something important, and if things went as well as he hoped then perhaps tonight they'd be celebrating her accepting his proposal.

He wanted to be with her—he'd made no secret of that. He'd declared his intentions to her several times, even though he'd felt a hint of reticence on her part, but whatever that part was, seemed to have been removed and she was ready to talk to him. She was starting to trust him again. This was good.

No sooner had he entered the house than a sudden ear-splitting scream pierced right through his heart.

'Rosie!' He dropped the flowers and his briefcase on the floor and rushed up the stairs. 'Rosie?'

There was no answer. Rosie knew that whenever he or Gwenda called her she must answer immediately. This time she did not respond.

Virgil hurried into her bedroom, his eyes scanning the floor. The bookshelves had fallen, trapping Rosie underneath. Virgil's heart hammered in his throat as he quickly bent and began tossing books out of the way before he could successfully remove the wooden shelves.

'Rosie?'

He heard Gwenda calling. 'In here,' he called back, and soon the housekeeper was by his side, helping to remove the debris.

'My goodness! Rosie! I was bringing in the washing, then coming to get her ready for her bath, when I heard that crash.'

'She must have climbed up on the shelves and overbalanced,' he surmised as he was finally able to reach his daughter.

He stopped himself from instantly scooping her into his arms, even though that was exactly what he wanted to do. Instead he ran his hands gingerly over her bones, checking for breaks.

'Her leg feels broken. Get my medical bag from the car and I'll stabilise her before we move her.'

'Do you want me to call an ambulance?' Gwenda asked, wringing her hands in anguish.

'I'll be able to get her there faster. Just get my bag.'

Gwenda went off to do his bidding but he stopped her. 'Can you get me the children's paracetamol liquid first?'

'Of course.' Gwenda grabbed the medicine before going out to the car to get Virgil's medical bag.

Virgil brushed the hair from Rosie's eyes. 'Sweetheart? Rosie?' he soothed, but received no response.

He checked her pupils, took her pulse, made sure she didn't have any cuts or scratches.

'Blossom? It's Daddy,' he said, and this time her eyes flickered open for a brief second before closing again.

She started to whimper and Virgil's heart constricted in pain. He hated it when she suffered. Why hadn't he found the time to ensure those bookshelves had been secured to the wall? Why hadn't he taken better care of his girl? Because he'd been busy paying attention to Clara rather than doing the one thing he was meant to do—being a good father to his child.

'Where is it sore, baby? Does your head hurt?'

Virgil administered liquid paracetamol through a dropper. Rosie was still whimpering.

'Shh. It's all right, darling. Daddy's here. Everything's going to be fine.'

Through the multitude of emotions Virgil was experiencing, uppermost in his mind was fear.

If anything happened to Rosie...he didn't know what he would do.

Being a father meant the world to him. Rosie was the most perfect thing he'd ever had in his life. Even though his marriage hadn't been the happiest, Rosie had been the little ray of sunshine which had brightened his existence.

He was angry at his daughter for attempting to climb up the shelves—especially when she'd been told not to do it. He was angry with himself for not ensuring the shelves were better stabilised. He was thankful he'd arrived home just at the right time—that he hadn't been delayed at the hospital. He was cross with himself for having dallied in buying flowers for Clara. If he hadn't, he'd have been home sooner and Rosie would have been playing with him, rather than making mischief in her bedroom.

When Gwenda returned, Virgil splinted Rosie's tiny little leg. It was ridiculous to realise just how small she really was. Once the splint was in place, he fashioned a small brace from a tea towel and the newspaper he'd asked Gwenda to fetch, so he could use it as a cervical splint.

'Just in case she has some injuries I don't know about,' he muttered to Gwenda as he carefully scooped his little girl into his arms. 'OK. Let's get her to the hospital.' His tone was brisk, his body rigid, his jaw set. 'You'll have to drive, Gwenda. Rosie may have a head injury and for the moment she's comfortable in my arms, so the less she's moved, the better.'

'OK.'

Just as they stepped outside he saw Clara's car just turning into his driveway.

'Never mind, Gwenda. We'll go in Clara's car.'

Gwenda was already opening the rear passenger door. 'I'll lock up the house. then meet you at the hospital,' the housekeeper told him.

Virgil only heard half of what Gwenda was saying as the majority of his attention was focused on Rosie. When Clara took in the situation, Virgil briefly registered the look of horror on her face.

'No, no, no! What's happened to Rosie?'

'Some bookshelves fell on her.' Virgil's words were clipped and direct.

'Right. Straight to the ED for us.'

As Clara drove, she had to stop herself from speeding, from taking unnecessary risks to get Rosie to the hospital sooner. Virgil simply sat there with his daughter in his arms, crooning over and over.

'Shh, baby. It's all right. Daddy's here. Daddy will fix everything.'

The anguish in his tone was veiled, but she heard it, and it broke her heart to see him in so much pain.

When they arrived at the hospital they were met by an orderly with a barouche. Clara had called ahead, with her hands-free phone, to let the hospital know of their imminent arrival.

'I need X-rays of her left femur and, more importantly, her head.' Virgil was giving orders. 'Clara, I've given her paracetamol but nothing else. Find out the correct dosage for a child of three and get her some analgesics.'

'Does she have any allergies?'

'No.' He paused for a second. 'At least none that I'm aware of. She's only three years old.' He shook his head, as though to clear it, then another round of instructions flowed from his mouth. 'Contact the children's hospital in Melbourne and organise for a paediatric orthopaedic surgeon to come here immediately. The less Rosie is moved, the better,' Virgil instructed as he walked with the barouche into the hospital and through to X-Ray.

Clara wanted to soothe him, to tell him that everything would be all right, that children were resilient, but she wasn't sure of anything right now. It was becoming increasingly difficult to hold on to her professionalism because she loved that little girl so very much, but she knew she needed to stay cool, calm and collected—especially as it appeared Virgil was in full parental panic mode.

She didn't blame him. Instead, she did as he'd suggested and checked on the analgesic dosage requirements for a three-year-old, estimating Rosie's weight. Next she placed a call to the children's hospital in Melbourne and spoke with the director of Orthopaedics. She related the particulars of the accident and enquired whether a surgeon would be able to come to Loggeen for review.

'I'm sorry, Dr Lewis. I can't possibly spare anyone today.'

'The patient is Rosie Arterton. Virgil Arterton's daughter,' she added hopefully.

She knew Virgil would have friends in high places and at the moment he needed every string that was available, pulled.

She heard the director groan with frustration. 'Is there any sign of head injury?' he asked.

'She's being X-rayed now and has been slipping in and out of consciousness.'

'I don't know what else I can do. I'm sorry, Dr Lewis, I can't possibly spare anyone to send to Loggeen. Believe me—if I could, I would. Best to get her flown here in the hospital's helicopter and we'll ensure she's seen immediately.'

Clara sighed and the director picked up on it.

'I know he's not going to like it, but it's the best I can do.'

'Thanks. I appreciate it.' She rang off, then set about organising the helicopter. Once the transfer details were taken care of, she called Gwenda.

'Oh, how is she?' Gwenda sounded distressed.

'She's in X-Ray. We'll know more soon. Have you left home yet?'

'Just about to get in the car.'

'Would you mind packing some clothes, please? One

bag for Rosie—pyjamas and comfortable clothes—and also one for Virgil.'

'Why? Why? What's happened?' Gwenda choked back a sob.

'I can't get a specialist to come here so I've arranged a transfer for Rosie to the children's hospital in Melbourne.'

'Oh, no. *Oh, no.* I should have been watching her.'

'Gwenda, you can't be expected to watch her twenty-four hours a day. She'll be as right as rain.'

Even as she said the words Clara was trying to force herself to believe them. It all depended on the results of Rosie's head X-ray. If the little girl had suffered a concussion, or fractured her skull, things might take a turn for the worse.

'Oh, Clara, I hope so. How's Virgil?'

'Feeling helpless.'

'That's not good. OK, I'll go back inside and pack them both a bag.'

'Thanks. They'll be leaving in about half an hour, and at least the helicopter flight won't take too long.'

Clara rang off and reviewed her check-list to ensure she'd done everything that needed doing. She then called through to Radiology to check on Rosie's progress and was told that the little girl was being wheeled back to the Emergency Department.

Clara readied a treatment room and when she saw the orderly pushing the barouche, directed him into the room. She had analgesics ready for Rosie.

'What's the situation?' she asked quietly.

He turned and looked at her, his eyes wild. She'd never seen him looking so utterly helpless. He wasn't here as a surgeon in command—he was here as a father. There was nothing he could do medically to help his daughter and it was tearing him apart.

Seeing him standing outside his home with the small,

limp girl in his arms had caused an instant panic to ripple through her. The two people she'd come to love and
cherish were both hurting—one in physical pain and the
other in emotional anguish. She wanted to do whatever
she could to help.

'Head X-ray shows a small hairline fracture. I want a
CT scan performed to rule out any further injury. I'm still
waiting to see the X-rays of her legs. They said they'd email
the scans as soon as possible.'

'I have an injection for her.'

Clara set down the sterile kidney dish she'd used to
carry everything in. She opened the swab, unwrapped the
needle and drew up the shot. Swabbing Rosie's right thigh,
she injected it into the fatty tissue.

'There you are, darling.' Clara spoke softly once she'd
finished. 'That will help with the pain.'

Rosie's eyes fluttered open at the sound of her voice.
The child looked at her for a minute, quickly scanned the
room until she saw Virgil, and then closed her eyes again.
Clara felt a lump appear in her throat. Rosie was so vulnerable, so helpless. All Clara's suppressed maternal in-
stincts came bursting out. 'Everything will be all right.
Just sleep for now.'

Tears sprang to her eyes. So this was how a mother felt
when her child was ill. It was devastating—heart-wrench-
ing and unbearable. No wonder Virgil didn't want to leave
her alone. After everything he'd been through, Rosie was
his life. She looked at him, trying to convey the fact that
she understood his feelings.

He was watching his daughter, his jaw clenched tight.
'When will the surgeon arrive?' he asked.

'She has to go to Melbourne, Virgil.'

'No.'

'I spoke with the director of Paediatric Orthopaedics.
I told him it was your daughter but he can't spare any-

one. He's asked for her to be transferred by helicopter and promises she'll be seen immediately upon arrival.'

'No,' he reiterated. 'I will not allow her to be moved again. She's in too much pain. She needs a CT scan.'

Clara counted to ten. 'Virgil,' she said firmly, 'I understand how you're feeling—'

'You have no *idea* how I'm feeling,' he responded vehemently. 'You're not a mother. You don't have children of your own. How could you *possibly* understand how I feel? This is my *daughter*, Clara. My own flesh and blood.' He pointed to where Rosie lay. 'My daughter is lying there with a head injury, broken bones and in pain and there's nothing I can do.'

He ground his teeth, having spoken his words with determination.

Clara tried to let his words wash over her—he was worried about his daughter, after all—but the way he looked, the way he was gesticulating with his hands, his whole manner was reminiscent of how he'd been all those years ago at the fundraising dinner, when he'd told her that nothing else mattered in life but his career.

She forced herself to breathe calmly. Although his mannerisms might be the same, this was a different situation. He was worried about his daughter.

Still, he had no idea of the anguish he was causing *her*, Clara. No, Rosie was not her own flesh and blood. Clara would never be able to have any children of her own. But she had taken heart in the knowledge that if she loved Rosie enough, that would be all that mattered. She loved the child, rejoiced in her, and needed those childish little smiles to make her life complete.

'I may not be a mother, Virgil, but that doesn't mean I don't understand this situation. I love Rosie as though she were my own. I, too, feel devastatingly helpless, but in this situation you have to do what is best for your daughter. A

surgeon can't be spared from the children's hospital in Melbourne and therefore, Rosie must go there to be treated.'

'You have no right—' he replied coldly.

'I have *every* right,' she told him sternly. 'I'm the admitting doctor. Rosie is my patient. You're her parent—
act like it.'

Clara held Virgil's piercing gaze, not allowing herself
to be daunted by it. When he didn't immediately reply,
she took that as a sign that he was now willing to co-operate with her.

'The helicopter leaves in twenty minutes. Gwenda is
on her way here with clothes for you and Rosie. You'll no
doubt be at least three to four days in Melbourne before
Rosie can be transferred back here. I'll ensure your clinics and operating lists are postponed until you return.'

At the end of her speech she stared at him, holding his
gaze, her chin raised in defiance, almost daring him to dis-
pute her words. Virgil's answer surprised her. He stepped
forward and pulled her into his arms, holding her tight for
three seconds, burying his face in her neck. Then he let
her go just as abruptly.

Was that his way of thanking her? Accepting that she
was in charge? Being grateful for her support? She had no
idea what was going on in that mind of his.

'Are you coming to Melbourne with us?'

'Just for the transfer.'

Virgil clenched his jaw. 'What about in Theatre?' he
asked. 'If she needs surgery, will you stay for that? They'll
let you in.'

Clara knew what he was getting at. She wasn't a blood
relation to Rosie and could therefore be admitted into theatre as an observer.

'If they agree, I'll be there. I love her, Virgil.' Clara's
words were soft and tears began to brim in her eyes. 'I love
that little girl with all my heart, soul and mind.'

'I can see that.' Virgil sighed, and she hoped his previous panic was over. He looked over at his little girl and shook his head sadly. 'She's so helpless and I can't just snap my fingers and make it better. I hate it when she's not well. It's my worst nightmare coming true.'

'Let me check and see if those scans of her leg have come through,' Clara said, and walked to the nearest computer screen. Sure enough, the digital scans were there, and together they looked at them. 'Greenstick fracture. The bone's bent on one side and splintered on the other.' Clara clicked on a different file and looked at the X-rays of Rosie's cranium, where a small hairline fracture was visible. 'I've already booked a CT scan for her in Melbourne,' Clara remarked, after they'd reviewed all the different scans.

'So she *will* require surgery.' He exhaled slowly as the situation sank in.

'It's minor, Virgil, and the operation to realign the splintered part of the bone back into place, takes less than thirty minutes. Slap a plaster cast on her leg and she's done.'

'She's never had a general anaesthetic before.'

His tone was soft, and for the first time since he'd bundled himself and the small child into her car, Clara was talking to the real Virgil.

'I'm sure she'll be fine. Kids are resilient. It's the parents who end up going grey with all the worry and stress.'

Clara crossed to his side and brushed her fingertips through his hair, delighted that he wasn't pulling away from her any more. As though he sensed her need, he reached for her with his free hand, the other one still firmly holding his daughter's.

'Come closer,' he urged, and when she complied he pressed his lips firmly to hers, his kiss filled with apology. 'I'm sorry,' he whispered. 'I said some awful things to you. Forgive me?'

Clara sighed and brushed her fingers through his hair once more. 'I don't scare that easily any more,' she replied, and kissed him back, wanting to show him that she'd already forgiven him.

CHAPTER TWELVE

Rosie was given a general anaesthetic for the CT scan. She needed to be absolutely still, and the machine was rather frightening—even for some adults. As Clara had predicted, everything was fine except for the small hairline fracture which had shown up on the X-rays.

She quickly reported the findings to Virgil, who visibly relaxed and sank into a chair. Gwenda had insisted upon coming with them to Melbourne, which meant Virgil wouldn't be left alone with his thoughts while Rosie was in Theatre.

After the CT scan, the next step was to realign Rosie's leg. Seeing Rosie's small body, limp with anaesthesia, almost made Clara want to weep. It was different when a child was sleeping—a natural, healthy sleep rather than being sedated. She'd seen it on countless occasions with other patients but this was *Rosie.*

Get a grip, Lewis, she instructed herself as the theatre staff prepared for the operation.

It proceeded without a hitch, and Clara managed to switch off her feelings and observe the techniques the orthopaedic surgeon used. Finally the cast was in place, and Rosie was being wheeled to Recovery. Clara went with her, holding her hand as they went.

'Clara.' Virgil came into Recovery and crossed to her side, his face anxious with worry.

'She's fine, Virgil. The procedure went well, with no complications, and she'll make a complete recovery.'

Clara released her hold on Rosie's hand and stepped back, allowing Virgil access to his daughter.

'She really is all right?'

The statement was made with astonishment, as though he'd expected something terrible to happen.

'She's fine.'

Clara took a few steps away from Rosie's bed and Virgil looked at her.

'Where do you think you're going? I want you here—with Rosie.'

Clara smiled, delighted to hear those words from him. 'You stay with her. I'll go tell Gwenda the good news.'

'OK, but don't be gone too long. Once Rosie comes round, I'm sure she'll want to see you.'

'"And then my heart with pleasure fills, and dances with the daffodils!"' She quoted Wordsworth to him and he smiled.

'Go and tell Gwenda our little girl is fine. I'll try and talk the recovery nurses into letting her come in.'

'I'm sure you will, Virgil.'

Clara laughed. He was back. Her lovable, caring and silver-tongued darling was back.

When she told Gwenda the good news the other woman's face instantly relaxed and she breathed out with relief.

'She's really OK?'

Clara chuckled and nodded. 'She really is.' Clara beckoned for Gwenda to follow her. 'Virgil is going to try and smuggle you into Recovery. After all, you're like another grandmother to her, and she'll want you close by.'

Sure enough Virgil had squared it with the nurses.

'But only for two minutes.'

'Two minutes is all I need to see that she really is OK.'

With Gwenda and Virgil by Rosie's side, Clara was starting to feel the area was a little crowded and, not wanting to make the Recovery nurses angry, she excused herself.

'I just need to check something,' she murmured before leaving Recovery.

She left Recovery and walked down a long corridor towards the front of the hospital. The late evening warmth surrounded her as she breathed in deeply, grateful that Rosie was all right. The sky was a blend of glorious colours and she forced her mind to settle down to a more normal pace. She stared at the sky, just absorbing the moment—something she'd learned to do during that long year of recovery—but knew she'd soon need to start making arrangements for her return to Loggeen.

'Hopefully,' Virgil said to her a while later as she bent to kiss Rosie's forehead, 'we can transfer her back to Loggeen tomorrow some time.'

Rosie had been moved out of Recovery and onto a ward. Gwenda was sitting in a nearby chair, passing the time by knitting, and Virgil was keeping a close watch on his daughter.

'Children do tend to recover so much quicker than adults, and if the doctors are happy with her progress then that's a definite possibility,' Clara agreed. 'But you take care, too, Virgil. Don't go skipping meals or sleep. You won't do Rosie any good if you do. Doctor's orders.' She pointed her index finger at him for emphasis.

'You're not my *doctor*,' he replied as he released his hold on Rosie's hand and placed his arm about Clara's waist, drawing her closer. 'You're my *fiancée*.'

Clara raised her eyebrows in surprise and then looked across at Gwenda, who had stopped her knitting.

'Did you hear that, Gwenda? I'm supposedly Virgil's fiancée.'

The older woman's lips twitched as she tried to hide a smile.

'Forgive me for pointing out one small flaw,' Clara continued, 'but you haven't actually *asked* me to marry you—ergo, I can't possibly be your fiancée.'

'A small oversight.' He shrugged. 'The fact remains, though, that I *do* want to marry you, Clara. So what do you say?'

She started at him, aghast. 'What? That's it? *That's* my proposal?' she asked incredulously.

'Well, it's not exactly the way I planned it,' Virgil responded, scratching the side of his head.

'Good—because I don't accept *that* proposal.'

His answer was to chuckle, and she sighed with relief. Seeing him less stressed was a good thing.

'Why don't I walk you to the helicopter and you can tell me what your answer might be when I *do* propose to you properly?'

'Checking to see I'm going to give you the answer you want?' she asked as they left Gwenda to keep an eye on Rosie.

'I may be impatient, Clara, but I'm not a complete fool. Of course I'm checking. What man proposes if he knows the answer is going to be no?'

As they got into the lift to head towards the helipad, Virgil slipped his arm around her waist, his tone soft as he spoke.

'I know we have a lot of things to discuss, but I'm sure we'll get there, Clara. You love me. I love you. Everything else is—irrelevant.'

'Virgil...' Her eyes were wide with concern. 'I hope that *is* the case because—'

'Shh.' He bent his head and placed his lips briefly on hers. 'It can wait. Everything will be fine—trust me.'

Once they stepped out, a cool breeze whisked around them. Now that the sun had set, the evening had become rather cool. Floodlights lit the area and the helicopter pilot gave Clara the thumbs-up when he saw her. He proceeded with his pre-flight check and she took the opportunity to say a proper goodbye to Virgil.

'Please keep me up to date with any changes, good or bad, in Rosie's condition?'

'Will do,' he promised, drawing her closer. 'You take care, Dr Lewis. We'll have that talk as soon as we can.'

Then, before she could say anything, he simply lowered his head and captured her lips with his.

The kiss was soft and gentle and yet filled with promise. The warm, masculine scent of him swirled throughout Clara's body and she sighed with relief. As the wind began to pick up slightly, Virgil gathered her closer, protecting and shielding her from its coolness.

Clara's heart pounded with love for him, and the knowledge that her feelings were reciprocated only intensified her own. Virgil loved her, and yet there was a niggling doubt in the back of her mind that refused to budge, and it was that which was causing her the most consternation.

'You love him. He loves you. I don't understand why the two of you aren't announcing plans for your future life together,' Arthur stated the following evening, when Clara and Juzzy went over for dinner.

'Arthur, things aren't always so cut and dried,' Maybelle said, her words pointed. 'Remember with us… We loved each other but there were other things to sort out first.'

Arthur sighed as he passed the salad bowl to his sister. Clara helped herself but then looked down at her plate, unsure she'd be able to eat the delicious meal her brother had cooked.

'What is the one thing that's really troubling you?' Maybelle asked, after watching Clara push her food around on her plate for a minute or two.

'The *one* thing?' Clara looked at her sister-in-law. 'I guess it was when Rosie was sick, and he looked at me with such disbelief that I could actually love her so much even though she wasn't my own flesh and blood. I *do* love that little girl.

Later, as Clara tucked Fuzzy-Juzzy into her doggy bed and went to brush her teeth, she started to count her blessings. She enjoyed good health, had a roof over her head, a good job, a loving dog and a family who stood beside her, no matter what.

But what she wanted was to have Virgil—her soul mate—in her life on a permanent basis. She wanted to adopt children so Rosie could know and understand the love of a sibling. She wanted Gwenda to enjoy being a grandmother to all those children, and she wanted to fill a house with love and make it a home. *Their* home. Hers and Virgil's.

Was it wrong to want so much?

Three days later, after sporadic short phone calls and many text messages, Virgil, Gwenda and Rosie were back home, the little girl apparently quite excited to have her leg in a purple plaster cast.

'She wants you to come over and write your name on it, and for Juzzy to put her pawprint on the cast,' Virgil said over the phone.

'That'll be…interesting. I can just imagine Juzzy stepping into a tray full of paint and then running around the place, leaving pawprints on everything *but* Rosie's cast.'

His answer was to chuckle, and the warm sound washed

over her, causing the love she felt for him to burst forth
within her again. No matter what his reaction might be to
what she had to tell him, her heart would be his for ever.
This was something she'd come to terms with over the
past few days. She loved Virgil. One hundred per cent.
And that meant she would either have a very happy life
with him or a lonely one without him. For now, though,
she was through living in limbo.

'Listen, are you free right now? My last patient has
cancelled so I'm done for the day and, well… I need to
talk to you.'

'I'm free,' he told her, but she thought she heard a note
of concern in his tone.

Was he worried about what she might say? Or was Clara
simply borrowing trouble yet again?

'Do you want to come to my place? See Rosie? Have
dinner?'

'Actually, why don't you come to *my* apartment. We'll
be less likely to be disturbed.'

'Fingers crossed no emergencies come in,' he stated.
'I'll be at your apartment in about twenty minutes. I just
need to finish writing up some paperwork.'

'Sounds good. See you then.'

And she rang off before she could change her mind.

Twenty-five minutes later Clara was pacing around her
apartment, wondering if something had happened to him.

'Where is he, Juzzy?' She opened the front door and
checked the hallway again, but there was still no sign of
him. Telling herself not to panic, she re-straightened the
cushions and checked her phone for the hundredth time
just in case Virgil had sent her a message. Nothing.

Thirty-five minutes later there was a knock at her door
and she opened it, her eyes wild and filled with worry.

'Hi!' Virgil stood there, smiling at her, and all Clara

could do was throw herself into his arms and press her mouth to his.

Given she hadn't seen him since she'd left Melbourne, he was most definitely a sight for sore eyes.

Their mouths knew exactly how to respond to each other, how to entice and excite. Clara shivered involuntarily and sighed as he continued the sweet torture, shifting them both slightly so they weren't standing in the doorway. Clara kicked the door closed with her foot before deepening the kiss. She loved him so much and wanted him to feel every ounce of that love. She wanted him to be secure in the knowledge that together they could accomplish anything.

Virgil's rough five o'clock shadow tingled lightly over Clara's face as he broke free and pressed small kisses all the way around to her ear. 'This is so right,' he murmured. 'We belong together. We've always belonged together.'

It was such an exact replica of her own thoughts that she marvelled at how in tune they were with each other's feelings.

She led him to the lounge, holding his hand in hers.

'Before you start, can I just say that I'm really happy you're trusting me with whatever it is you need to tell me?'

Clara nodded and let his hand go, her palms beginning to perspire with her increased anticipation. 'I have something to tell you. And I'd like you to remember while I tell you that I love you.'

'Clara?' He frowned at nervousness. 'This is *me* you're talking to. We've worked through so much. We can deal with whatever comes our way.'

'Oh, Virgil, I hope so.'

Clara swallowed a sob, trying to summon the courage to confess the truth. He went to envelop her in his arms but she held up a hand to stop him.

'No.'

She needed to see his face when she told him the news, to try and read his initial reaction. The best way was the most direct—just blurt it out. And blurt it out she did.

'Virgil, I can't have children.'

There—she'd told him. The millisecond of relief she felt was squashed by the immediate devastation that crossed his face.

'What? How?' he questioned. 'But I know you want children, Clara, and I know you love Rosie, so—'

'I do, Virgil.' She clasped her hands to her chest, covering her heart. 'More than anything in the world I would love to have a child to grow within me, but it's medically impossible.'

As though the penny had dropped, he stared at her for a moment. 'The car accident.'

'My pelvis was so drastically crushed that I had to have a hysterectomy and unilateral oophorectomy. The remaining ovary isn't in good shape either, and was only left so I didn't go directly into menopause at such a young age.'

She bit her lip, willing him to speak, to say something, but he remained silent, as though trying to take in everything she was saying.

Finally he cleared his throat. 'That evening when we went for the picnic—'

She nodded. 'I wanted to tell you but I didn't know how. I know you want more children, Virgil, but I...I...can't.' Clara choked on a sob. 'And I want you to know that even though I'm not Rosie's biological mother—I'll never be *anyone's* biological mother—I love her so very much, as though she really were my own. I *love* her, Virgil, and I hope that together you and I can raise her and love her and perhaps provide her with—with siblings in another way.'

'Adoption?'

She tried not to wince at the way he spoke the word, as though it were ludicrous.

'Or we could use a surrogate. Perhaps one of the reproductive specialists can find one good egg of mine and fertilise it and—'

'What?'

He was looking at her as though she'd grown an extra head. Clara wrapped her arms about her waist, glad she was sitting down, because the look on his face of utter disbelief at the realisation of what her words meant, was making her feel faint.

Virgil stood and walked over to the bookshelf, where there were several pictures of Clara and her family, but she could tell he wasn't seeing any of them. His mind was whirring, trying to compute what she'd told him.

Eventually the surrounding silence became too much for her to bear.

'Say something. Please?'

Virgil dragged in a breath and turned to look at her, raking his hands through his hair in agitation, as though he had no clue what to say or how to deal with the bomb she'd just dropped.

'I'll be honest with you, Clara. I'm stunned. Your injuries must have been utterly horrific. I mean, you told me you'd sustained a pelvic fracture as well as other trauma, but to have to deal with something like this as well...'

He trailed off, and Clara wasn't sure whether it was a good or bad thing that he was processing just how extensive her injuries had been. The question she needed an answer to was whether or not he'd be willing to try and have a family with her in the not so usual way.

He was looking at her now as though he was waiting for her to say more.

'Er...my accident... Right... Well, it was a good twelve months before my gait was back to almost normal, but my surgeons were happy with my progress.'

She wanted to add that it could have been worse—that

she could have ended up in a wheelchair or even lost her life—but the physical trauma of her accident had been dealt with and she'd moved on. Hopefully Virgil would be able to move on with her.

He raked a hand through his hair once more, looking adorable and cute and so sexy and… And then she realised he was shaking his head in a negative way.

'I…er…I need to go.'

Clara closed her eyes, desperately trying to hold back the tears—tears which were only the tip of the iceberg when it came to the heartbreak she was presently feeling.

'I need to think,' he ventured, obviously feeling the need to twist the proverbial knife he'd just thrust into her heart.

He didn't make any attempt to hold her or kiss her or anything, but instead walked to her front door, opened it quietly and left.

Clara clamped both hands over her mouth in an effort to hold in the heartbreaking sobs which threatened to burst forth. She didn't want him to hear her crying. She didn't want him to see how his words, his actions, had ripped her to shreds once again.

She collapsed back onto the sofa, curling up into the foetal position and giving in to the pain. The old feelings of helplessness and heartbreak returned as the tears fell.

Juzzy—beautiful Juzzy—came and curled herself instantly in her mistress's arms. Clara held on to the dog as she sobbed. She had always yearned to be a mother, and with Rosie she'd been given that opportunity. Now it would all be taken away from her.

No friend in Gwenda.

No daughter in Rosie.

No soul mate in Virgil.

She was alone—again.

CHAPTER THIRTEEN

THE RINGING OF the phone pulled her from the deep sleep she was in and for a moment Clara had no idea where she was. The only thing she knew for sure was that she was very uncomfortable.

Opening her eyes, she realised she was still curled up on the sofa. Fuzzy-Juzzy had clearly decided to go and eat at some point, because she could hear the dog lapping from her water bowl.

The phone continued to ring. Sitting up, she groaned as her muscles protested at the position she'd contorted them into. Her mobile was on the coffee table in front of her.

'Hello?' she mumbled, her throat dry and scratchy. 'Dr Lewis.'

'Clara.'

Virgil's deep voice rumbled down the line and Clara almost dropped the phone.

'Virgil,' she whispered. All coherent thought left her as their discussion the previous evening, came flooding back.

'Clara—we need to talk.' He was direct and to the point. 'I know it's early, but can you come over before you head to work? Rosie would love to see you,' he added as an incentive.

Anger burst forth within her. 'Don't use Rosie as an excuse. I think it's best for Rosie if I don't see her again.'

'I can understand your anger—' Virgil ventured, but Clara interrupted.

'Oh, you can, can you? I don't think so, Virgil. Do you have *any* idea how hard it was for me to open up to you? To trust you? To tell you about something which has caused me years of distress? I saw a therapist for well over two years post-accident, because I wasn't able to deal with the fact that I might never become a mother, and then…and then you come back into my life and I think… Well, actually it doesn't matter what I thought, because all you've done is prove to me that you haven't changed at all. You're still that same man who put his own agenda in front of my happiness all those years ago.'

'Now, wait a second—' he started to say, but she cut him off.

'I have nothing more to say to you, Virgil.'

She was about to disconnect the call when his words tumbled out in a rush.

'Wait. I was an idiot. I love you, Clara. Please?' he implored. 'I handled everything badly. I'm sorry. I'm so sorry. Please, come over?'

Clara was silent. She'd never heard Virgil so worried, or so desperate.

'Please? Don't deny me the chance to explain.'

She looked at the clock. If she got ready for work and skipped breakfast she could make it to Virgil's, hear him out, and still make it to the clinic in time.

'I'll be there in an hour.'

'But—'

'An hour, Virgil.'

'An hour's time. See you then.'

His pleasant tone was forced and she rang off, her hands trembling with anxiety. Was she doing the right thing?

Clara dragged in a deep breath and stood, commanding her legs to hold her weight. She reminded herself that she was a strong, independent woman, and if she needed to live the rest of her life without Virgil Arterton, then she would.

'How much longer, Rosie?' Virgil was asking the little girl as they sat playing on the floor with some blocks. 'How much longer?'

Gwenda had let Clara into the house and told her that Virgil and Rosie were in Rosie's bedroom. Virgil had his back to her, playing intently with his daughter, mindful of the plaster cast on the little girl's leg.

Clara's heart swelled with love for him at seeing the caring and patient attitude he displayed with Rosie. He loved that little girl so much—surely he could extend that love to any other children they might have.

He built up a tower and Rosie knocked it down with her hand. Then her little blue eyes spied Clara in the doorway and her face radiated happiness.

'Clara!' she squealed, and instantly tried to stand, the cumbersome plaster cast making it difficult.

'Stay still, sweetheart,' Virgil told Rosie as Clara tiptoed her way through the toy debris scattered around the place.

She crouched down next to Rosie, wanting to keep a bit of distance between herself and Virgil.

'Hello, sweetie.' She gave Rosie a kiss. 'You're looking so much better.'

'You're here.' Virgil put out a hand to touch her. 'I'm not imagining it?'

The light touch on her upper arm caused a burst of fiery awareness to flood through her. She did her best to ignore it. 'I'm really here, Virgil.' She tried not to put too much inflection into her tone.

Rosie clutched at Clara's hand. 'Let's have a special playtime with Daddy. Let's play with the blocks. I know the letters. That's an A,' Rosie announced, holding up the appropriate block. 'That's a G,' she told them earnestly.

'Can you build a tower?' Virgil asked. 'Get Clara to help you,' he decided. 'I bet she loves building towers.'

'I do,' Clara declared, and together she and Rosie built a big tower and let it fall to the ground. Blocks went everywhere and Clara started to gather them up again, delighting in the child's giggles.

That was when she realised what Virgil was doing.

He'd arranged some of the blocks to spell out a message.

Clara was immediately thankful that she was already sitting down.

There, in multi-coloured plastic blocks, he'd put the letters together to spell out WILL YOU MARRY ME?

Clara could only stare at the letters, her eyes beginning to blur with tears. She looked at him, and then at Rosie, who seemed oblivious to the adults, then back to Virgil again.

'I'm sorry, Clara,' he whispered, and took her hand in his. 'It came as a shock and I didn't handle it well. If we can't have any children, that's fine. We have Rosie but, more important, we have each other.

Clara appreciated what he was saying, but did he really grasp the concept? 'If we adopt a child,' she asked slowly, 'do you think you'll be able to love that child just like you love Rosie? A child that isn't biologically your own?'

Virgil instantly nodded. 'Yes.'

There was no hesitation in his answer, and that helped to alleviate some of Clara's tension.

'What I said to you when Rosie was in the hospital—that you couldn't know what I felt like because you weren't a mother—that was mean and cruel and I'm so incredibly sorry. My only defence is that I was beside myself with worry for—'

Clara leaned over and pressed a finger to his lips to stop him, tears brimming on her lashes. 'It's OK. I accept your apology.'

Virgil took her hand in his and gazed lovingly into her eyes. 'I have thought about what you've told me, and I've reflected on what you've been through and how, when you met Rosie, you simply accepted her and loved her. It was so natural and easy for you, and it made me realise that you deserve to be a mother. You and me, we deserve to be parents together. And Rosie...' He looked at his gorgeous girl. 'She deserves to be loved by both father *and* mother. Together—the three of us—we can make that happen, and if there are any other children who join our family then it will make us all richer in love.'

His words were heartfelt and sincere and Clara found it difficult to control her tear ducts.

'Please, Clara, marry me? We've been through so much and yet we've found each other again. It's meant to be. Please be my partner. Be Rosie's mother.'

Virgil tenderly wiped the tears from her eyes, a look of hope in his. Clara looked at the blocks, unable to believe this moment was finally here and that he was waiting... waiting for her answer.

'Clara?'

The word was filled with worry, and it was enough to help her to snap back to reality. Smiling, she reached out her free hand and gathered three of Rosie's blocks together, arranging them to spell her answer.

'Y... E... S...' Rosie read the letters out, then blended them together. 'Yes! It says yes!' Rosie clapped her hands with delight that she'd read a real word.

Clara looked at the little girl and kissed her. 'Yes. That's exactly what it says. It says yes.' She looked at Virgil. 'Yes, I'll marry you.'

A slow smile spread across Virgil's lips and his eyes were alight with love as edged closer, needing to kiss her immediately.

'Kiss Rosie, too, Daddy,' the little girl interrupted, and Virgil laughed.

Clara laughed too as he complied with the wish of the other female in his life. Clara felt incredible—on top of the world—and it was all because of the two people in front of her.

'Clara is going to come and live with us,' Virgil told Rosie.

'Yippee!' Rosie announced loudly.

'My sentiments exactly.' Virgil nodded.

EPILOGUE

'Rosaleen Cait Arterton...' Clara warned in a voice her daughter had come to learn and respect over the past three and a half years.

'Yes, Mummy?' the six-and-a-half-year-old asked innocently.

'You've been told countless times before not to climb up on your bookshelves. Thank goodness your father bolted them to the wall after your previous fall or there would have been another injury.'

'Sorry, Mummy.'

'All right. Go and tell the twins to pack up their toys and wash their hands for dinner.'

'Do we *have* to pack up? We love playing together. We'll be quiet. We won't wake the babies.'

Maybelle came into the dining room carrying a large bowl of salad. 'It's not a matter of waking the babies,' she told her niece. 'It's a matter of dinner being ready to eat. And if the girls don't listen to their big cousin, tell them their mummy will come and check on the state of the playroom and it had better be tidy.'

'Yes, Aunty Maybelle.' Rosie sighed again and headed off down the hallway, grumbling about how difficult it was to be the eldest.

Clara turned to Maybelle and both of them chuckled. 'Such a hard life.'

Clara walked over to where a large travel cot was set up in the corner of the room. Snuggled inside were two little babies. It had taken some time for the adoption process to happen, and when she and Virgil had been notified that there was a baby waiting for them in the Pacific Island nation of Tarparnii, they had been surprised to find the adoption was for twins.

'We know all about twins,' she'd said as they'd accepted the offer, thinking of Arthur's gorgeous girls. 'Double the blessing, double the love and—'

'Double the trouble,' Virgil had stated.

And so they'd been blessed with two baby boys.

That had been four months ago, and now both Eddie and Percy had finally settled into something of a routine.

'When I have baby number two,' Maybelle said, rubbing her enlarged abdomen, 'do you think Gwenda will help me?'

Clara laughed. 'I don't know how I would have coped without Gwenda. While Mum and Dad are more than happy to spend time with their grandchildren, they also like to travel. Besides, as far as everyone's concerned Gwenda's another grandmother.'

'And I love each and every one of my grandchildren,' Gwenda stated as she brought more food out to the table.

She came over to join Maybelle and Clara, watching the twins in their cot. The two boys, with their dark skin and big brown eyes, had captured everyone's heart.

'My cup really does run over,' Clara murmured.

'You and me both,' Maybelle added.

'I'll join that club,' Gwenda chimed in, and the three women embraced, knowing that even though they might not be biologically related they were family through and through.

'Right. Enough of this soppy stuff,' Gwenda said a moment later. 'I hope that Arthur and Virgil are done cooking on the barbecue outside. Why men persist in shooing women away from the barbecue, I don't know. I can cook on it much better than either of them.'

Gwenda headed off to check on Arthur and Virgil while Clara bent to pick up Eddie, who was starting to fuss.

'I'll go check on the progress of the crazy cousins,' Maybelle said.

'I might give Eddie his bottle before we eat.'

'Good idea.'

Maybelle headed off towards the playroom and Clara cuddled her son close. She'd just sat down with a warmed bottle, Eddie drinking hungrily, when Percy started to cry.

'*Ugh.* You boys. You always tag team.'

'I've got him.'

Virgil's deep voice washed over her as he came into the room.

'Dinner's ready, by the way, but I'll organise a plate of food for you and put it aside.'

'Thank you.' She smiled as she watched him pick up Percy, kissing the baby's head before holding him close. Percy instantly stopped grizzling as his father held him, as though glad he was finally getting some attention.

Virgil came and sat down next to Clara, watching Eddie drink his bottle of formula.

'I love our boys, Clara, and they are *our* boys. We've only had them a few months and yet I can't remember life without them.'

'They complete our family.'

'That they do.' He leaned over and kissed his wife's lips. 'You, me, Rosie, Eddie, Percy, Gwenda, Fuzzy-Juzzy and Peachy the bird.'

'And in another four months—' Clara nodded to where Arthur was standing behind his wife, his hands resting on Maybelle's pregnant belly '—we'll add to that number again.'

'It doesn't bother you, seeing Maybelle pregnant?' Virgil asked softly.

Clara instantly shook her head. 'After everything Maybelle's endured, she deserves a world of happiness.'

'And that, Mrs Arterton, is what we all seem to have found.' He kissed her once more, as though he couldn't get enough of his wife.

'*Ugh!* Why do you always have to do that kissing thing?' Rosie asked as she looked across at them.

Their daughter was sitting up at the table next to her cousins.

'Yeah,' one of Arthur's daughters added. 'Our mum and dad do that too.'

'*Blech!*' the three of them said in unison, making all the adults laugh.

'If you eat your dinner quickly,' Clara told Rosie, 'you can feed Percy.'

'OK.' Rosie's attitude instantly changed as she started to spoon food onto her plate. She loved helping with her baby brothers.

'We're going to be big sisters too,' stated Samantha, one of Arthur's twins.

'And we're going to help Mummy and Daddy with our new baby,' added Kristen, the other twin.

'You bet you'll be helping,' Arthur agreed, winking at his daughters.

'We're all going to help each other,' Maybelle stated, and raised her glass of apple juice in the air. 'I'd like to make a toast. Everyone get a glass.'

It took a good three minutes before everyone had a glass with something in it so they could make a toast.

'To family. Both here and those travelling. May we always support each other with unconditional love, never asking why but instead asking, What can I do to help? I've been so blessed since I came back into Arthur's life, and never in my wildest dreams did I think I could be this happy and this cherished.'

'And never in *my* wildest dreams,' Virgil added, tacking his own bit onto Maybelle's toast, 'did *I* ever think I would be married to the woman I love the most, and that we would have an incredible family.'

'To family,' Clara said, clinking her glass with Arthur's.

'To family!' everyone echoed.

'Can I eat now?' Rosie demanded, and they all laughed.

* * * * *

*If you enjoyed this story, check out
these other great reads from
Lucy Clark*

*REUNITED WITH HIS RUNAWAY DOC
ENGLISH ROSE IN THE OUTBACK
A FAMILY FOR CHLOE
STILL MARRIED TO HER EX*

All available now!

MILLS & BOON®
Hardback – October 2017

ROMANCE

Claimed for the Leonelli Legacy	Lynne Graham
The Italian's Pregnant Prisoner	Maisey Yates
Buying His Bride of Convenience	Michelle Smart
The Tycoon's Marriage Deal	Melanie Milburne
Undone by the Billionaire Duke	Caitlin Crews
His Majesty's Temporary Bride	Annie West
Bound by the Millionaire's Ring	Dani Collins
The Virgin's Shock Baby	Heidi Rice
Whisked Away by Her Sicilian Boss	Rebecca Winters
The Sheikh's Pregnant Bride	Jessica Gilmore
A Proposal from the Italian Count	Lucy Gordon
Claiming His Secret Royal Heir	Nina Milne
Sleigh Ride with the Single Dad	Alison Roberts
A Firefighter in Her Stocking	Janice Lynn
A Christmas Miracle	Amy Andrews
Reunited with Her Surgeon Prince	Marion Lennox
Falling for Her Fake Fiancé	Sue MacKay
The Family She's Longed For	Lucy Clark
Billionaire Boss, Holiday Baby	Janice Maynard
Billionaire's Baby Bind	Katherine Garbera

MILLS & BOON®
Large Print – October 2017

ROMANCE

Sold for the Greek's Heir	Lynne Graham
The Prince's Captive Virgin	Maisey Yates
The Secret Sanchez Heir	Cathy Williams
The Prince's Nine-Month Scandal	Caitlin Crews
Her Sinful Secret	Jane Porter
The Drakon Baby Bargain	Tara Pammi
Xenakis's Convenient Bride	Dani Collins
Her Pregnancy Bombshell	Liz Fielding
Married for His Secret Heir	Jennifer Faye
Behind the Billionaire's Guarded Heart	Leah Ashton
A Marriage Worth Saving	Therese Beharrie

HISTORICAL

The Debutante's Daring Proposal	Annie Burrows
The Convenient Felstone Marriage	Jenni Fletcher
An Unexpected Countess	Laurie Benson
Claiming His Highland Bride	Terri Brisbin
Marrying the Rebellious Miss	Bronwyn Scott

MEDICAL

Their One Night Baby	Carol Marinelli
Forbidden to the Playboy Surgeon	Fiona Lowe
A Mother to Make a Family	Emily Forbes
The Nurse's Baby Secret	Janice Lynn
The Boss Who Stole Her Heart	Jennifer Taylor
Reunited by Their Pregnancy Surprise	Louisa Heaton

MILLS & BOON®
Hardback – November 2017

ROMANCE

The Italian's Christmas Secret	Sharon Kendrick
A Diamond for the Sheikh's Mistress	Abby Green
The Sultan Demands His Heir	Maya Blake
Claiming His Scandalous Love-Child	Julia James
Valdez's Bartered Bride	Rachael Thomas
The Greek's Forbidden Princess	Annie West
Kidnapped for the Tycoon's Baby	Louise Fuller
A Night, A Consequence, A Vow	Angela Bissell
Christmas with Her Millionaire Boss	Barbara Wallace
Snowbound with an Heiress	Jennifer Faye
Newborn Under the Christmas Tree	Sophie Pembroke
His Mistletoe Proposal	Christy McKellen
The Spanish Duke's Holiday Proposal	Robin Gianna
The Rescue Doc's Christmas Miracle	Amalie Berlin
Christmas with Her Daredevil Doc	Kate Hardy
Their Pregnancy Gift	Kate Hardy
A Family Made at Christmas	Scarlet Wilson
Their Mistletoe Baby	Karin Baine
The Texan Takes a Wife	Charlene Sands
Twins for the Billionaire	Sarah M. Anderson

MILLS & BOON®
Large Print – November 2017

ROMANCE

HISTORICAL

MEDICAL